TWO LOVERS, SIX DEATHS

A gripping crime thriller full of suspense

GRETTA MULROONEY

JOFFE
BOOKS

Published 2016 by Joffe Books, London.

www.joffebooks.com

ISBN 978-1-911021-95-7

For Grainne, dear friend and skilled reader.

CHAPTER 1

He had stabbed her as she lay sleeping. Days later, he had taken his own life, leaving a written confession. These were the facts in the newspaper lying in front of Tyrone Swift.

> Dominic Merrell, 39, was found hanged on Monday evening at his place of work, the Hays hotel in Southwark. He left a signed confession, stating that he carried out the bloody and brutal murder of his girlfriend, Lisa Eastwood, in their home three days earlier. Merrell hanged himself from a wardrobe door. Police have indicated that they are not looking for any other suspects. Merrell leaves a wife and two children.

There were two photos on either side of the article. On the left was a stunning woman with long corkscrew curls and a wide, beautiful smile. One of those perfectly proportioned faces, exquisite in its harmony. On the right was a man with an open, dreamy expression, a pronounced cleft in his chin, dark-rimmed glasses and floppy brown hair. A pleasant, average face.

Swift observed the gaunt woman sitting across from him. She had arrived at his basement office looking exhausted but composed and had maintained her self-possessed air until now. Her name was Georgie Merrell. She was the man's wife and the bringer of the newspaper on his desk.

'This tells a compact story,' Swift said. 'Your husband hanged himself, presumably through remorse and guilt. He confessed to murdering Ms Eastwood. From what I read, the police are accepting his confession.'

'Exactly. But it isn't true. Dominic didn't do it, he couldn't have done it.' Her mouth began to tremble and she put her hand over it.

'You know, things are sometimes just as they seem,' he said softly.

He rose and poured her a glass of water. She held it in both hands and sipped. She was extremely thin. She had a pale, freckled face, free of make-up and with finely shaped, bloodless lips. Her long brown hair was drawn back from her bony forehead into a narrow plait that fell to her waist. He thought she must be in her late thirties but she looked older, worn down by cares. She had a contained, attentive expression, which made him think of nuns in their wimples.

'I've come to you,' she said, 'because I remembered reading that you found out who had attacked that boy in Epping Forest all those years ago. I was looking up private investigators and when I saw your name, it rang a bell. Then I looked at your website and saw your considerable experience. The police aren't going to do anything.'

'Why don't you believe that your husband murdered this woman?'

'Because he was a kind, decent, soft-hearted man. Somewhat gullible, maybe, but he had no violence in him. He couldn't watch brutality in films or anything involving blood. I knew him, Mr Swift. We were together for many years and in that time we rarely argued, and he was always loving and gentle towards his children and me. He didn't have it in him to attack anyone, especially not a woman.'

Swift knew that everyone had the potential for violence but that luckily, most people never found cause to release it. He could see why the police were taking no further action. They had plenty of unsolved murders to keep them busy without questioning the confession of a man who had saved them the cost of a trial. He rested his head back in his deep office chair and crossed his long legs. Georgie Merrell's freckles stood out against her pallid skin.

'You speak very generously about your husband. Presumably, he left you for Ms Eastwood. Abandoned wives aren't usually sympathetic to their exes.'

She pressed her lips together and nodded. 'You're right. How can I explain? When Dominic left me, over two years ago, I was devastated and angry. I stayed that way for some time. But in the end, I still loved him. I love him now. He was the man who cried with me over our miscarriage, who was my rock when my mother died, and rubbed my temples for me when I had a migraine.' She stopped, swallowed. 'We married young, at eighteen. I thought we would be together always, into our old age. We have two sons. I don't want them to grow up believing that their father was a murderer. What mother would want that for her children? They have already come home from school saying that other pupils are calling their father a killer. Someone drew a noose in one of their books. My eldest son has deleted his Facebook and Twitter accounts because of . . . of disgusting comments. He got into a fight with someone about it, came home with a cut lip but he wouldn't discuss it. People can be so thoughtless, so cruel.' She stood and walked to the window, looking up through the security bars at the small paved front garden. Her angular figure was that of a teenager, her legs like twigs in her close-fitting jeans.

Swift stifled a yawn and rubbed his eyes. He had returned that morning from visiting an old friend in Lyon, an ex-colleague from the days when he had worked for Interpol. He had walked, rowed for hours on the wide rivers Rhone and Saône, drank Bière Blonde and eaten well. His return flight had been severely delayed and he had been confined with a crowd of other frustrated travellers in a small, hot departure room at Lyon airport with tantalising glimpses of aircraft taking off outside. He'd had little sleep and had arrived back just half an hour before Ms Merrell turned up for her appointment. He was still readjusting to work mode and was aware that he needed a shower.

Ms Merrell drew her plait over her shoulder and held it for a moment, then turned and sat down again.

'Dominic didn't do this terrible thing,' she said softly.

'Then why did he confess and then kill himself?'

'I don't know. I just don't know and it is tormenting me. Something dreadful clearly happened to Dominic but I have no idea what. I am left with questions that go round and round in my head. My sons are distraught. They are angry with their father, all over again. He has abandoned them twice. Adam keeps telling me that his dad couldn't have done it. What can I say to him? Words seem meaningless. It hurts when you can't comfort your children, make things better. It seems the very least a parent should be able to do.'

Swift glanced again at the newspaper she had given him. 'This took place about eight weeks ago. When did you last see your husband?'

'A fortnight before, early January. He usually took the boys, Harry and Adam, out twice a month. Well . . . that's what used to happen but then Harry refused to see him sometimes and he just took Adam. But Harry did go with them on that last Saturday and they went for a pizza and saw a film.'

'Why did Harry refuse to see him?'

'He wouldn't say. I would guess anger, disappointment, feelings of betrayal. I'm not sure Harry himself understood why.'

'How did your husband seem on that Saturday?'

'He was okay. A bit tired, I thought. I only saw him briefly. He didn't come in. Lisa often kept late hours. I understand she was a social animal. Dominic was a shift engineer, employed by Hays hotels, so he had to work some nights.'

'Did you know Lisa well?'

She gave a wry smile. 'Not well at all, but I introduced her to Dominic. I made her an unwitting gift of my husband. I do pet portraits, you see, mainly from photos. I have a little studio at home. Lisa contacted me because she wanted a portrait of a guinea pig. She posted the photograph. I met her just once when she called by to pick up the finished picture. She was very friendly and warm so we chatted for a while. I remember thinking how beautiful she was. She had a kind of glow. She told me the portrait was a surprise for an elderly friend's birthday. It seemed a considerate gesture, bothering to think of something so personal. Dominic came in as we were talking and the next thing I knew, a couple of months later he was leaving us.' She shook her head. 'I've heard before about men becoming involved with women their wives know. Why is that?'

'Laziness and proximity coming together with opportunity?' Swift suggested.

She sighed. 'It was a possibility that had never occurred to me. You see, Dominic was clearly head over heels in love with Lisa. Stricken, stunned, swept off his feet. She was very lovely. I could say that she enchanted him and I think there is some truth in that. I think she made a habit of enchanting men. I hoped at first that it was an infatuation, that he would come to his senses and come back to us. But after a while I had to accept that he was committed to staying with her.'

Georgie Merrell interested Swift. She was distressed but appeared to bear little rancour or hostility towards the dead woman. He could detect the effort it had cost her to hold things together.

'Lisa had had other husbands or partners?'

'One husband, I believe. Other partners and one child, a daughter. I don't know where the child is, she didn't live with her and Dominic. I didn't want to know. I only know that much because Dominic told our sons a few details and they carried them home to me. That is one of the problems when children are involved in a split. They collect information for you, whether you want it or not.'

Swift pointed to the rings on her third finger. 'You and Dominic remained married?'

She touched the rings. He could see that she was close to tears but she blinked them away.

'I didn't want a divorce and he didn't press for one. As far as I know, Lisa wasn't interested in marriage. I think she might still have been married herself. Dominic rang to tell me that she was dead, you know. He sounded so odd and distant. I offered to let him stay with us because the police had sealed her flat off, but he refused. He didn't want to speak to the children. He put the phone down on me. That hurt.'

'He must have been in a strange state of mind. Where was he staying?'

'At the Hays hotel, where he died.'

'So neither you nor your sons saw him after the murder?'

'No. Not alive. I visited him at the funeral parlour. I put his wedding ring back on his finger, held his hand, sat with him, talked to him. I told him we loved him, always. We are comforting ourselves, aren't we, when we talk to the dead?' She swallowed and shook her head.

'Can I get you a tea or coffee, something stronger?'

'No, thank you. I'm fine with water.'

'Do you know of any friends of your husband that I can contact, people who might know more about his life recently?'

'Dominic had one close friend, Finbar Power. They had known each other since they were teenagers. He played squash with him and they went fishing sometimes. Finbar came to the funeral but other than that, I hadn't seen him since the split. I always got on well with him but he stayed in Dominic's camp. Divided loyalties, I suppose. One of my sons mentioned seeing him at Lisa's flat once. I have a phone number for him.'

'Anyone else? Your husband's siblings or parents?'

'Dominic's parents are both dead. He was an only child.'

'What about the home he shared with Lisa? Will I be able to see it?'

'I'm not sure. Dominic's things are no longer there. Lisa's father, Mr Eastwood, kindly allowed me to have his belongings collected. Lisa owned the flat and I believe her father is clearing it out. I suppose it will be sold but I don't know. I can give you his contact information. He lives in South Africa. I am sorry I can't tell you much more about Dominic's life in recent years. I am sure he had met other people through Lisa but when he left, I told him I didn't want to know anything about his new relationship. I kept the life he had chosen over us at arm's length. It helped me deal with the parting. He understood that and respected it. I know that he suffered because of the decision he had made. He was an emotional man, easily moved to tears and his family was important to him. It just shows how strong his feelings for Lisa must have been.' She pressed her hands to her cheeks. 'So, when we saw each other we talked briefly about the boys and financial arrangements, practical things like that.'

'You say you discussed money. Was he okay financially?'

'I don't know. He was contributing to the mortgage payments on our house. I don't make enough from my work to take it all on myself. He kept buying gifts for the boys. I wasn't happy about it but I couldn't stop him. He got expensive toys for Adam, a top of the range Vespa scooter for Harry. It was guilt, of course. I don't know if he paid Lisa rent. Dominic also gave me an agreed amount for our sons and he had a steady job. He was a steady man until he met her. He was my north star.'

There was a silence. She stroked her rings, appearing to be in a reverie. Swift made notes. He liked what he saw of this woman. She seemed convinced of her husband's innocence and her motives struck him as genuine. Swift doubted that there was much mileage in an investigation and it would be tricky. He would have to get to know two dead people through the subjective views of their families and friends. Information would be partial and biased. Their home and possessions, which could divulge evidence, were already being dismantled. However, the situation was unusual and would offer a challenge. His recent success in finding the perpetrators of a vicious attack on a young man had brought positive publicity. Swift's name had featured in the press with headlines of the *ex-cop private eye finds forest killer after fifteen years* variety. But the cases coming in since then had been workaday: tailing errant wives and husbands for suspicious spouses, an executive wanting dirt on a rival, an insurance scam.

Georgie Merrell looked up at him. 'God knows, I've cried an ocean of tears over Dominic and for a while I thought I hated him. But he loved that woman. He would never have harmed her. And he loved his sons. I don't know why he claimed responsibility for the murder. Please, will you at least ask some questions? If you come back to me and tell me I am wrong, I will shed more tears but at least I will have tried my best. My sons will know that I have and then maybe I can find a way to talk to them, help them.'

'Yes, okay, I'll take a look.' Swift took out a contract for her to sign and requested the usual deposit. 'How old are your sons?' he asked.

'Harry is eighteen, Adam is twelve.'

'I'll want to talk to them. I will be sensitive. I need to form a picture of how their father was around the time this happened.'

'Yes, that would be okay. I would like to be with them, though. Harry has taken this particularly hard. He hardly speaks at home. I just can't get through to him at all. It's as if someone exploded a bomb in our house and we are living in the ruins, in a daze, trying to pick up the pieces. Yes, that's how it feels. I've never had concussion but I think this is what it must be like.'

'I am sorry. I appreciate that coming to see me has taken a huge effort.'

'Thank you. You're kind.'

He hoped she would still think so if he ended up confirming her husband's confession.

'Do you have your husband's phone? Did he have a laptop or iPad?'

'Yes, I still have his phone although I've ended the contract so it's not in use any more. He didn't have any other devices. Adam knew the phone's security code. I looked at it but there was nothing I could see to explain what happened. Just emails about work. Harry looked too and said Dominic had cleared the call and search history before he died. He did clear emails and messages regularly as a matter of course. He was like that — neat, meticulous.'

Or perhaps concealing something.

She put down the pen, smoothing the contract. 'I always hoped that Dominic would come back to us one day. And he did, but in a coffin. Still, he was ours again at the end, with his family who love him around him, looking after him.'

'You've been through a very difficult time.'

She didn't seem to hear him. She had drifted away into her own thoughts again, her gaze meditative. He poured another glass of water for her and watched her drink it absent-mindedly.

When she had finished he saw her out, then made a coffee and googled the murder story for more details. He learned that Lisa Eastwood had thrown a party in her flat in Dulwich. Dominic Merrell stated that he had returned from a night shift around six thirty a.m. to find her in the living room, soaked in blood. She had been stabbed twice. A couple of days later, Merrell had taken his own life at his workplace. The manager of the Hays hotel said that Merrell was a reliable, honest and friendly employee who had worked for the company for many years and his colleagues were terribly shocked, etc. etc. A DCI Kharal was quoted as saying that there would be no further enquiries. These were sparse pickings. Even the tabloids told him little else, other than that Lisa was a vivacious Latin American beauty, probably because a confession drained the drama from the situation. There was another photo of her, a full-length shot with the Thames in the background. She was tall, slender, wearing a belted red leather coat. Her glossy dark hair had blonde streaks and flowed over her shoulders. Her eyes brimmed with laughter and confidence.

Swift considered which of his Met police contacts he should ring to get DCI Kharal's number. He didn't like to trade too often on goodwill so he varied his ports of call. He decided to phone DI Archie Lorrimer who he had worked with the previous year. He rang his number, got an answerphone and left a message.

He locked his office and headed upstairs to his flat. He showered, and then made cheese on toast. His cousin Mary had given him a coffee machine for Christmas and he inserted a pod and switched it on, listening to the satisfying hum. Spring was trying to get underway but the day was grey and bleak. Lyon had been cool but bright, with high blue skies, the sun almost warm at noon. His flat was still chilly from his absence. He turned up the heating and ate standing at the kitchen window, looking up at the fast moving cinder-coloured clouds and watery sun. He thought of Georgie Merrell's steadfast love for her dead husband, despite his betrayal of her trust. It took an extraordinarily generous spirit and stoicism to overcome abandonment as she had. Her visit had unsettled him in ways he found hard to deal with. His thoughts wandered to Kris, the woman he was still grieving for and to Ruth, who he still loved despite everything that had happened between them. He washed his plate, banishing memories, not wanting to visit those places in his head and heart where pain and confusion lurked.

* * *

Swift had finished stocking up on groceries along King Street in Hammersmith. The pavements were thronged, a pale sun encouraging shoppers. Taxi doors slammed, car horns blared, smells of baking and coffee wafted from cafés. Charity fundraisers in tabards tried to make eye contact, wanting to interest him in cancer, the homeless, UNICEF and donkey sanctuaries. An elderly woman pushing a shopping trolley full of her belongings tottered by, muttering to herself. Someone thrust a leaflet for a car boot sale at him. A woman accidentally sliced his ankle with a massive pushchair, smiling nervously as he winced and said not to worry.

As he turned towards the river, he heard the flute before he saw the player, a melancholy, slow melody drifting over the hum of traffic and high squeal of bus brakes. It sounded Arabic. The girl was standing near a kebab shop. A cardboard box at her feet contained a handful of coins. She was skinny, dressed in stained jeans and a grubby blue and red Arsenal sweatshirt with the logo Fly Emirates across the chest. Her hair, in a top knot, had a large, fabric, apricot-coloured rose securing it. The embellishment suggested resilience. Her playing was pure and sweet and she swayed, her fingers dancing. Because of this and because she was so thin and had a large orange-yellow bruise near her eye, Swift dropped a £2 coin in the box. The girl nodded, playing on.

As Swift neared his house, he saw Oliver Sheridan leaving. He was carrying a skateboard. They nodded to each other and Sheridan hefted his rucksack and snapped a twig from the hedge as he put his skateboard on the pavement and took off. He was wearing cut-off denim shorts and combat boots with yellow laces. He head was closely shaven and he had long bushy sideburns. Not an attractive look. Oliver was the obnoxious only child of Cedric Sheridan, Swift's dear friend and sitting tenant. Cedric lived on the top floor of Swift's house in a self-contained flat. Swift had inherited his friend with the house when his aunt Lily left it to him. They kept a benign eye on each other, and in return for the occasional meal from Cedric and loans of his car, Swift did the odd favour for his friend. In the past, this had included ejecting Oliver Sheridan from the house when he had visited in order to abuse and extract money from his elderly father. Oliver was a mediocre sculptor with grandiose ideas about his talents. Cedric maintained that Oliver had mellowed after spending six months in an artists' colony in Spain, but Swift reckoned this was wishful thinking. As far as he could see, Oliver was as moody and inconsiderate as ever. He visited Cedric whenever the fancy took him, to spin him yet another sob story about the hardships of the artist, milk his father's guilt feelings about his bitter divorce from Oliver's dead mother and to relieve him of money. Swift had crossed swords with Oliver Sheridan on more than one occasion. For the time being, they were on cautious nodding terms and Swift kept a watchful eye on him if he knew he was around.

He was unpacking his shopping when DCI Laith Kharal rang. Swift dropped a carton of milk as he grabbed his phone. It split as it landed at his feet.

'I hear you're asking questions about the Eastwood murder.' Kharal sounded surly.

'That's right. Thanks for getting back to me.' Swift explained that Georgie Merrell had engaged him to look into the case. 'She doesn't believe her husband could have committed a violent crime.'

'Families often find it hard to believe one of them is a murderer. But as you know, it's usually a relative who did it. So, if Merrell's innocent why did he leave a note?'

'I don't know. She was married to him for a long time and she's convinced he couldn't have done it.'

'And you believe her?'

'That's not the issue. It's too early for me to say. She is paying me to ask questions, so that's what I have started doing.'

'So, we conducted an investigation and we agreed with Merrell's confession that he'd done it. We told the families. End of.'

'I'm not questioning your investigation.' Not for now, anyway.

'Generous of you.'

'I'm doing a job. Mrs Merrell understandably doesn't want her sons to go through life believing their father was a murderer.'

Kharal's tone grew sarcastic. 'And you're taking her money. You're ex Met, aren't you?'

'Yes. People come to me with questions and I try to find answers. That's the nature of private investigation.'

'Hmm, private detective playing at being a police officer. Is that because you couldn't cut it in the real police force?'

Swift counted to six. 'Look, DCI Kharal, I don't need to explain to you why I set up my own business. In the last couple of years, I have sustained a fractured skull and a knife wound during investigations. I wouldn't call that "playing."'

'Yeah, well, let's not get into a pissing competition.'

'Let's not. I know you don't have to tell me anything. I don't want to trespass on your territory and I am not suggesting your investigation was lacking. Cut me some slack here. If I come up with anything, you will be the first to know and you can act on it. That wouldn't do your career any harm.'

There was a pause. 'Maybe. So, let's see. I can tell you what was in Merrell's note. It was short and sweet so I can remember it word for word: "*I killed Lisa. I'm sorry. Tell everyone how sorry I am."* There. That clear enough?'

'It's clear but it may not be the truth. Have you any other evidence that Merrell did it?'

'So many questions. Look, Archie Lorrimer says you're okay, but just because your cousin is an assistant commissioner in the Met doesn't mean you get free access to a murder enquiry.'

'I didn't mention my cousin. Okay, just bear with me. Merrell definitely committed suicide, no question?'

'Yep.'

'What DNA did you find at the flat?'

Kharal sounded highly amused. 'We were swamped with DNA, mate. There had been a massive party at the flat. The place was covered in sweat, fingerprints and saliva from dozens of people, and a dollop of vomit. Strong smell of wacky baccy. Oh, and a patch of semen in the bathroom where there must have been a knee-trembler.'

'Any defence wounds?'

'Nah. Stabbed twice in the left chest and stomach. Pierced the aorta, so she was awash with blood, all hers. Buckets of the stuff. Victim was lying passed out on the sofa when it happened, so drunk she probably didn't know much about it.'

'Weapon? Swift asked quickly.

'We didn't find it.'

'Did you suspect Merrell before he hung himself?'

'Possibly. He had some blood on him but he said he'd held her in his arms when he found her, so that ticked that box.'

'What kind of knife?'

'Small, thin, sharp. Now you're being cheeky. Sod off, I've got real police work to do.'

The line went dead. Swift uttered a 'sod off yourself, tosser,' and wiped up the milk puddle he was standing in. Lisa partied while Merrell was at work. He wondered if that had happened often and what it indicated about the relationship.

He jotted quick notes and a time line so far. He had worked in both the Met and Interpol before setting up Swift Investigations. These careers had honed his skills in surveillance, interviewing and scoping an investigation as well as some useful self-defence tactics. He thought that this tragedy had the potential to be a long and complicated enquiry. Finbar Power had known both Lisa and Merrell. Swift switched on the coffee machine and rang his number, then the manager of the Hays hotel.

CHAPTER 2

Swift had woken early and lay for a while thinking about a particularly satisfying row a few days before on the river Saône, stopping off in L'île Barbe to look at the ruins of the ancient monastery. In his mind he went through the trip, stage by stage, analysing and sifting the experience. He had completed one stretch at speed, the boat singing through the water. The air had been clear and clean, making his blood pump. He had been rowing since his teens and he became edgy and irritable if he didn't take his boat out regularly. The solitude and concentration invigorated him, put life into perspective. It had saved his sanity when his mother died — after Ruth left him — and when Kris was murdered — slowly piecing him back together. Rowing was a never-ending process of learning and re-learning, building up layers of experience. Like life itself. He enjoyed going back over a specific trip such as the one on the Saône, reflecting that his coordination and posture had improved.

He heard Cedric start the lawnmower outside and sat up. The back garden was small with just a patch of grass and Cedric kept it mowed to a fine tilth, starting early in the year as soon as it was sufficiently dry. He checked his email and saw that he'd had one from Ruth:

Dear Ty,

I hope you are okay and that business is good. I'm doing well, and so is our daughter. I had a check-up the other day and she is behaving perfectly. They confirmed that my due date is June 6. Not that long now.

I need to tell you that Emlyn got in touch with me and I have agreed to see him and discuss things. He was frank with me about what happened last year and he does feel bad about what he put you through and of course about Kris. He never intended that Kris should be harmed.

I can only say that he seems genuinely sorry. I think that the collapse of his career and the impending trial has made him focus on what matters in life. He wants us to get back together and give our marriage another chance. He says he understands that you will want to see your child and he is happy to negotiate whatever can be done to make this okay with you. I know that his illness makes him behave oddly at times but I do believe he is sincere. I have regrets too and I feel I owe it to him to talk these things over. He is still my husband and he will need support through the trial and afterwards, whatever the verdict.

Ty, I know how hard this is for you. It's hard for us all. I'll contact you when I have seen Emlyn.

R x

He felt a tide of anger rise at the mention of Emlyn Williams. He browsed back to the email Ruth had sent him in February, the one where she had told him she was staying with a friend near Barnstaple. It had the latest scan of their baby attached and he calmed himself by looking at the small nestling shape.

Sometimes he felt as if he, Ruth and Williams were locked in a grim dance, dragging themselves around a floor while a band played discordantly. Ruth had been his fiancée, the love of his life. Like Georgie Merrell and her steady faith in her husband, he had believed they would always be together. Ruth had met, run off with and married Emlyn Williams, a barrister, in the blink of an eye. Swift had met her again some years later. They had started seeing each other, sharing platonic lunches, and he had supported her through a miscarriage. Williams had developed MS and had become subject to fits of depression and anger. Swift and Ruth had slept together again just once, resulting in this pregnancy. Williams had discovered their meetings and had hired a petty criminal to harass Swift. This campaign had ended in the murder of Kris Jelen, the only woman Swift had felt any tenderness for since Ruth. They were just months into their relationship. Swift had been the one to find her body. Williams had been overjoyed when Ruth became pregnant again, and then furious when she told him that Swift was the father. Ruth had left Williams in great distress and Swift had not seen her since then. She had refused to say where she was until recently but had emailed him once a month to reassure him that she and the baby were okay.

Kris had been strangled and Williams, the man who had inadvertently caused her death, would probably end up with a suspended sentence, mainly because of his poor health. Now there was a strong possibility that he would be involved in this baby's life. Swift knew that Ruth felt a deep sense of responsibility towards her husband, that she had experienced conflicting emotions in recent months and might well return to him.

He showered and dressed in black jeans and a long-sleeved T-shirt. He forced himself to think calmly before replying to Ruth. Whatever he felt, however bitter and angry, Emlyn Williams was still Ruth's husband and the choice had to be hers. He waved to Cedric who was now filling the bird feeders, and sent an email:

Hi Ruth,

It's good to know that you and our little one are doing well. Your husband is difficult territory for me after what happened. It may well be that he regrets the outcome of his actions but they had irreversible consequences.

Let me know how your meeting goes. I think we should see each other soon to talk things through. I want to see you. It has been too long.

Ty x

What he really wanted to say was, *I know everything is a mess but in the end, you are and always have been the one. Come back to me and we'll see what we can salvage from the wreckage.*

He took coffee out to the garden for himself and Cedric and they sat side by side on the old swing seat in the watery sun. Cedric was in his late eighties but appeared remarkably youthful. This was partly due to his thick white hair and good skin but also his resilience in the face of life's vicissitudes. His favourite saying was *fall seven times, stand up eight.*

'Have you seen that young girl playing the flute near the kebab place?' Cedric asked him.

'Yes. She's good. I gave her some money.'

'Me too. Her name is Yana Ayo. She's from Aleppo in Syria.'

'A refugee?'

'Presumably. We spoke briefly but she looked a bit scared when I asked her about it, so I didn't press her. She's very thin, I'm sure she's malnourished.'

The next-door neighbour came out and started talking to her cat in a baby voice. The cat's name was Nigel and he was obese from all the cheesy treats he was given. This was bad for Nigel but good for the birds as he was too slow to catch them. Swift and Cedric exchanged glances.

'I heard from Ruth,' Swift said.

'She okay? And the baby?'

'Yes. She is talking to her husband. He wants them to get back together. He's remorseful about Kris.'

'Remorseful! That lovely girl . . . such a terrible, pointless waste of a life.'

'Yes.'

Cedric was quiet for a moment. 'My dear, if that happens, if Ruth goes back to him, he'll see more of your child than you do.'

'Exactly.'

Cedric touched Swift's hand briefly with his thin fingers, and sipped his coffee. Nigel clambered on to the wall and glared at them before waddling off to another garden.

* * *

Hays Hotels were a chain at the budget end of the market, scattered throughout London and the South East. They were purpose built, and their TV advertising featured three endearing bears who loved their beds and the pots of instant porridge provided in all the rooms. Gimmicky but memorable. Swift had established that after Lisa died, Dominic Merrell had spent three nights at the Southwark Hays. He had hanged himself on the third. Swift walked to the hotel from London Bridge. A sharp breeze blew off the river, ruffling his dark curls. A diminutive couple wearing identical bright blue jackets and huge backpacks asked him the way to the Globe theatre. He pointed, towering over them from his six feet three, saying it was just ten minutes' walk. They asked him to take a photograph of them posed against Southwark cathedral and he obliged.

The hotel was near Borough Market and Swift's mouth watered as he cut through the lines of stalls selling cheeses, breads and pastries, olives, dried fruits, spices, cured meats, paella, curries, fish soups and myriad other exotic dishes. He promised himself lunch soon.

The hotel manager, Dora Madibe, was waiting for him in the blandly beige reception area, where a notice proclaimed *Courtesy, Consideration, Calm*. They shook hands.

Ms Madibe wasn't quite as short as the couple he had just photographed but he felt like a giant again as he looked down at her small, heart-shaped face. She was wearing the Hays brand colours, pale blue skirt and a gold shirt with navy piping.

'As I explained on the phone, I'd like to see the room Mr Merrell stayed in and where he was found.'

'Yes, I've checked that it's okay. I must stay with you while you look, though.' She had a low voice, friendly. 'It's a small room we keep for staff in case of sickness or bad weather. I let Dominic stay there, given what had happened to his partner. It's in the basement, if you want to follow me.'

They took the lift down. He followed Ms Madibe past a kitchen and laundry rooms and along echoing tiled corridors busy with staff pushing trolleys of sheets, towels and cleaning materials. Swift noted the gold and blue pots of porridge with their pictures of the three satisfied bears on one trolley. Ms Madibe swiped her card on a door and preceded him into a narrow, windowless room with a single bed, a chair, a tiny bedside table, and tall fitted wardrobe. She stood against the cream wall, hands folded in front of her.

'Please, do look. There is nothing here. The police took Dominic's bag. I believe they were going to give it to his wife.'

Swift looked in the drawer of the table and the wardrobe. They were empty, apart from half a dozen hangers in the wardrobe.

'Where was he found?'

'I found him. He was hanging from the wardrobe door. He had used some thick cord. He attached it to one of the hooks inside.'

'I'm sorry. It must have been a terrible shock.'

She nodded, her face tightening. 'Yes. I've been in the hotel business long enough to have dealt with some difficult situations and one other suicide — sleeping pills.

That was a female customer and she looked peaceful. This was harder because I knew the person. Hanging is more violent, too.' She crossed to the table and switched on the air conditioning above it.

'Where was the note?'

'On the bed, written on our notepaper.'

'Did you read it?'

'Oh yes. It wasn't in an envelope. I knew not to touch it, of course. It just said that he had killed Lisa and he was sorry.' She shook her head, her tightly woven braids swinging, the orange and black beads clicking softly.

'What did you think?'

She sat on the edge of the bed and gestured to the chair. Swift sat. The room was stuffy, cell-like, and he was glad that the air conditioning had kicked in. He looked at the bare, featureless walls and thought that the place would depress you even if you weren't already sad.

'I found it hard to understand. Dominic was such a nice man, very kind. He wasn't always based here, you understand. He travelled between our hotels around London, doing maintenance work. He'd been working here quite a lot since Christmas because we'd had problems with heating and electrics.'

'How long had you known him?'

'About five years. He had worked for the hotel chain a long time and he had a solid reputation. I always found him polite and hard working.'

'So he was working here when his partner died.'

She had candid eyes and a slow, careful way of speaking. Swift could see her calming any troubled waters on her shift.

'Yes, that's right. Dominic had done an overnight shift. It's often easier to deal with maintenance that affects the main systems then. He came in at ten p.m. and finished at 6 a.m. He rang me that afternoon to tell me what had happened and to ask if he could stay here for a few nights.'

'You didn't find that strange? Usually someone would have friends or family to go to in a crisis.'

'I thought it was a bit sad and I didn't think this room was the best place for him. I wanted to help him in any way I could. He was very upset, obviously, and I didn't want to ask too many questions. I assumed he had nowhere else to go.'

Yet his wife had offered him a sanctuary with her and their children. Interesting that he had chosen this solitary, cheerless place.

'How did he seem, during those days he stayed here?'

'Deeply upset, quiet. He wasn't working. We gave him compassionate leave. Nobody saw much of him, to be honest. I came down to see him on the second evening, just to check he was okay. He said he didn't need anything. He was sitting on the bed and he looked . . . he looked like a man living a nightmare. He said very little to me, just that he had seen too much and everything was his fault. I could see he didn't want to talk. He looked so pale.' She frowned. 'Though I would say that he seemed a bit low in himself for a while before all this happened.'

'In what way?'

There was a clatter in the corridor and a shout. She rose and stepped outside, holding the door ajar, speaking to someone and asking them to clear up as quickly as possible. Swift rarely found a chair that was substantial enough to accommodate his long legs. He shifted, imagining Merrell lying on the bed, staring at the off-white ceiling, listening to the drone of the air con, seeing a woman covered in blood.

Ms Madibe came back in. 'Sorry, one of the staff had overloaded a trolley. More haste, less speed.'

'You were saying Mr Merrell had seemed a bit down.'

'Yes. It's hard to describe, really. He just seemed preoccupied at times. He was a quiet person anyway. His work was fine.'

'Was he friendly with anyone in particular here?'

'I don't think so. He was courteous to everyone but he just got on with the job. He liked his work, and he would get absorbed in it. The staff were terribly shocked when they heard about his death. The nature of his work meant that he was always moving from one hotel to another so he didn't really form friendships, and of course our staff change frequently. I wouldn't know about the other hotels.'

'How many are there?'

She responded instantly. 'Twenty-six.'

'Did Dominic Merrell strike you as a man who could commit murder?'

'He was the most unlikely murderer I've ever met. You know, you get a sense of someone and he was genuine, thoughtful.'

Swift rose, handing her a card. 'Thanks for your time. Please get in touch if anything else occurs to you.'

She nodded. 'I went to Dominic's funeral. Those poor boys. A parent's suicide must leave a lasting mark.'

The market was bustling and full of noise as Swift crossed back through. The smells were heavenly, sour, sweet, and pungent. Steam rose from a spit holding a roast hog. He was spoiled for choice to satisfy his empty stomach as he sauntered between the stalls. Thai, Vietnamese, Balkan, Indonesian, Spanish, Ethiopian, Italian, Egyptian and French dishes — even sausages from Lincolnshire — were all on offer. In the end, he settled for Caribbean, a jerk chicken and salad wrap with a spiced carrot juice. He took his food into the grounds of the cathedral and sat on a bench, watching the world go by, wondering why Dominic Merrell had seemed preoccupied and down and why he had thought everything was his fault. Had he been regretting leaving his wife and suffering the remorse of a murderer or was there something else?

He had a couple of hours before his meeting with Finbar Power. He entered the cathedral and took a seat, enjoying the thought that Shakespeare would have spent time there. Shakespeare's brother, Edmund, was buried somewhere within. There was a free concert of Danish music underway and a racing polka was setting legs tapping. Tourists and locals passed in and out quietly, some stopping for a few minutes to listen. This was one of the many things that Swift loved about London: people of all nationalities and ages coming and going, hearing something surprising, something stimulating that lifted the spirits. So it would have been for centuries. A trio of violins started a slower, lilting air, a sweet tune.

* * *

Finbar Power owned a shop called *Johnny Dory* near the Angel. According to his website, he sold tropical and freshwater fish and he had told Swift he lived in a flat above the shop. Swift avoided the dank confines of the tube as much as possible so made his way there on two buses. An Atlantic storm had arrived, the strong wind was whipping through the streets and lifting garbage from the gutters. A crisp packet had attached itself to the bus window and fluttered before flying away in the next gust.

The shop was a large, softly lit room filled with tanks. Power was dealing with a customer when he arrived. He broke away to invite Swift to look around, saying he wouldn't be long. Swift examined the tanks of wriggling, vibrantly coloured creatures. There was an eye-catching polka dot fish called a Peppermint Plecostomus and a beautiful black and yellow feathery-tailed one, a Queen Arabesque Pleco. It was an expensive hobby. Most of the fish were priced at around forty pounds or over. The quiet environment, the gentle light and the smooth gliding of the fish were soothing. Swift was sure his blood pressure had dropped.

'This is a very calming place,' he said as Power saw his customer out and came up to him.

'Isn't it? I notice people tend to lower their voices when they come in. I certainly find it quiet after being a

25

trader in the stock exchange. D'you want to come up to my place for a cup of tea? I've put the *closed* sign up.'

'Thanks, yes.'

'It's through the back of the shop.'

He led Swift through to a small back office. There was a door set into the wall, opening on to a flight of steep stairs.

'You need to mind your head,' Power warned him, ducking as he went through. He was as tall as Swift, who wondered if he ever forgot to bend and cracked his skull.

He showed Swift into a living room at the back of the property and vanished to make tea. The room was painted white with pale green furnishings, the floor a whitish-grey wood. Stylish wooden framed armchairs stood around a glass-topped coffee table by the French window that looked out onto the garden. There was an iron balcony outside the window and metal steps down to a patio. There were no pictures or TV. The place was immaculate. Clinical, almost.

Swift's eye was drawn to an elegant aquarium that ran most of the length of one wall. The glass was rimless and ultra-clear and sat on a white, laminated cabinet. Tropical fish in glowing yellow, topaz, orange, scarlet and many hued stripes darted amongst rocks and ferns in their silent, illuminated world. A bookcase held books dedicated to fish and copies of *National Geographic*.

Power came in with a tray of tea and a plate of thin biscuits. He was slim but well built, with flaxen hair receding in a V-shape from his temples. His eyes were an intense blue, deep set. In the full light from the windows, he looked tired and pasty. His jeans and shirt were immaculate and expensive looking, his watch a Philippe Patek. There must be serious money in fish. The tea was proper too, leaves poured from a pot through a silver strainer. It was black, slightly aromatic.

'This is delicious,' Swift told him. 'Lovely flavour.'

'It's Vietnamese. I think they produce the best tea. I think you'll appreciate my easy chairs too. They're made for long legs.'

'I do.' Swift accepted a cinnamon biscuit. It melted on the tongue. 'As I said on the phone, I've come about Dominic Merrell. His wife can't believe that he murdered his partner and has asked me to take a look at what happened.'

'Poor Dom. The whole thing has been a nightmare. I still can't take it in.' He spoke quietly, his voice laden with sadness. He broke a biscuit into two pieces and shifted the crumbs around.

'I understand you were a close friend. I am sorry for your loss. Tell me about him.'

'I'd known Dom since we were thirteen, when my family moved from Limerick to Stamford.'

'He grew up in Lincolnshire?'

'That's right. My dad worked for an Irish bank and they were opening a branch in Stamford. It was quite a culture shock on all fronts. Limerick was a shabby, raucous, bustling city and Stamford is gracious and peaceful, something of a backwater to a city boy. I was lonely for a while, felt that I stuck out like a sore thumb. This was in the early nineties, when being Irish in rural England attracted some vitriol. Might still for all I know, although I think Polish and brown-skinned people have now taken over the status of worrying incomers. Stamford seemed very quiet and strange. I found it hard to read people. No one invited you into their home. I met Dom my first day at school and we clicked. He and his parents were friendly, very open, asked me round for tea straight away. We became best mates. He was a lifebelt for me, really. We used to go fishing together. I have him to thank for my enduring passion for the world of fish.' He smiled sadly and sipped his tea.

'It sounds as if you'd been in contact ever since.'

'That's right. We both left school at sixteen. I came to London to seek my fortune. I didn't quite believe that the streets were paved with gold but as it turned out, I did become a wealthy man here. Dom worked in Stamford for a while, then London beckoned or him too. I encouraged him to make the move and he got an apprenticeship as an electrician. We shared a small bedsit in Manor Park for six months. I joined a large investment firm, studied economics at night classes and worked my way up. Dom and Georgie met when they were seventeen, so I've known her for a long time too. I suppose not a month went by in all those years without Dom and me meeting. Once he met Lisa, it was a bit less frequent. He liked to be with her as much as possible.'

'Do you think he killed Lisa?'

The response was immediate. 'No, not for one minute, and I can't understand why he said he did. It doesn't make any sense. Nor does killing himself.'

'Did you see him after the murder, before he committed suicide?'

'Yes. He rang me and told me Lisa was dead. We met at a pub at Blackfriars, had a pint and a sandwich. He hardly ate, but I suppose that's not surprising. I offered him a bed here but he said no. He said he'd prefer to stay at the Hays, told me he needed to think about what he'd seen.'

Power had an immobile face that gave little away but his eyes were watery and filled with sadness, his voice tight with emotion.

'Did he talk about finding Lisa?'

'He talked a lot for Dom. He cried too. I had never seen him cry before. A kind of dry crying, awful. The police had been interviewing him and he was exhausted but he seemed to want to go over it. He said he had come home about half six and saw Lisa on the sofa. She often slept there after a party. It was dark in the flat and he thought she was asleep at first and went to kiss her. He said he put his hand in her blood before he realised she was dead. It was everywhere, he said, an ocean of blood, soaked right through the cushions and there was a puddle of blood on the floor. He put his arms around her and held her for a while. Said he knew that once he called 999, she would be taken away and never be his again. I remember he said, *there was a never-ending nightmare of blood and horror.* He repeated that a couple of times. He seemed stunned, to be honest, out of it. We just sat in silence then. It's hard to find words to say to someone in that situation, no matter how well you know them. I was so sorry for him.' Power took a tissue from his pocket and blew his nose. He rubbed his eyes with the heels of his hands.

Swift left a pause. 'That was the last time you saw him?'

'Yes. Then Georgie rang to tell me what had happened.' He shook his head. 'I still haven't taken it in. I can't take it in. It's all unreal.'

'Mrs Merrell said she'd lost contact with you after her husband left.'

Power held his hands out. 'You know how it is. You feel that you have to stay loyal to your friend. I was very fond of Georgie. I was best man at their wedding. It was difficult but in the end, Dom was my friend first and I couldn't see a way to stay in contact with her too without making things awkward for him. Dom never asked me not to see Georgie, he wouldn't have done that.'

'What did you think of him leaving his wife?'

Power looked at him, then out of the window, holding in emotion.

'Well, he's gone now so words can't hurt him. I saw how mad he was about Lisa and I could see why. She was very beautiful, charismatic. When she walked into a room, it lit up. It all happened very fast, him getting together with her. Too fast. He didn't really know her. I didn't know anything about it until he had moved into her flat. I thought he was playing out of his league, maybe having some kind of mid-life crisis. I never said that to him. You can only be so honest with your friends if you want to keep them.'

Swift finished his tea, savouring the last mouthful. 'Can you be more specific? Out of his league in what way?'

'Every way. Look, Dom was an average bloke. Bright, but normal. He had no great ambitions in life. He qualified as an electrician, and then joined Hays hotels. He stayed for years in a steady marriage. I didn't see that much of Lisa but she came across as a lovely social butterfly and a dreamer with a rich, indulgent father. She had flitted from one relationship to another and had all kinds of notions about exploring life to the full. I got the impression that meant exploring men to the full as well. She did love Dom, for a while anyway, but I don't think loyalty and settling down was her thing.'

'She was unfaithful to him?'

He took a breath, linked his fingers together and cracked the knuckles. 'I would think so.'

'Did he think that?'

'I reckon he suspected it but he didn't want to believe it. He had too much invested in her. He worshipped the ground she walked on. She could do no wrong in his eyes. There is a song with lyrics to that effect, isn't there?'

'You mean *When a Man Loves a Woman.*'

'That's it. Percy Sledge. It goes on about how a man would leave his best friend if he criticised the woman. So I was careful. He meant too much to me and anyway, I don't believe in interfering.' His eyes filled again. 'Sorry. I don't usually blub.'

'That's okay, you don't need to apologise.'

'It's just that I've been thinking back to Stamford, all the good times we had together. Things I had forgotten, happy times just messing around, fishing and swimming, having conker fights, cooking sausages on a fire by the river. Innocent. It's just as well you don't know what the future holds.'

'Grief often unlocks memories.'

'Yes. They are great memories. All I have of him now. Sorry, mustn't get soppy, that doesn't help you.'

'You presumably went to Lisa's flat sometimes. I believe Dominic's sons saw you there.'

He looked relieved to be released from his recollections. 'A couple of times, if Dom and I were hitching up to go fishing. I picked him up in my car. Harry and Adam were there once, so I had a chat with them. I could see that Harry was uncomfortable. He was almost sixteen when Dom left, at an age when you start judging your parents. Adam was more accepting of Lisa, more able to blur the boundaries. At least, that's how it looked. You never do know.'

'How about socialising with them as a couple?'

'I went to a few of Lisa's parties. I think Dom wanted a friend there, so I obliged. Parties aren't really my thing, I prefer to be at home reading or out fishing. Some of her friends were pretty wild. The place used to rock.' He shook his head. 'Dom looked so out of place at those parties. Like someone's dad trying to be cool. Not his style at all but he desperately wanted to please Lisa, fit in with her. Hang on to her.' He blinked fresh tears away.

A light step sounded on the stairs and a voice called, *Hallo!* Power stood up as a woman came in. She had short, dark hair and wore a pinstripe business suit and carried a briefcase.

'Louise, this is Mr Swift. Mr Swift, my partner, Louise.'

Swift rose and shook her hand. She had a friendly but intense expression and inquisitive eyes.

'Mr Swift has come to talk about Dominic,' Power told her. 'There might be a cup of tea left in the pot although it's probably a bit tepid by now.'

'That's okay, thanks, I've had a lot of coffee today.' She pulled a chair up next to Power and linked his arm solicitously. 'How are you feeling today, darling? You still look a bit worn out.'

'Better, thanks. I've had a virus of some kind, can't shake it off,' he told Swift.

'Anyway, don't mind me. As you were,' Louise said with a high-pitched laugh.

Swift addressed himself to Power again. 'So, given what you were saying, what did Lisa see in Dominic?'

'She was genuinely in love with him, I think. Maybe she was between partners and there he was. His steadiness probably attracted her. He made her laugh. She liked that. But you see, I think she fell in love easily and often.'

Louise snorted. 'She liked the fact he idolised her. It's an aphrodisiac to that kind of woman.'

Swift sensed an antagonism that might be useful. 'You knew Lisa then, Louise?'

'I met her a couple of times. She was full of herself, thought every man found her fascinating.'

Power looked uncomfortable and patted her hand. Louise moved in even closer to him. Swift thought she might soon hop into Power's lap.

'Well, Dom certainly found her fascinating,' Power said.

'Had you noticed any changes in Dominic in that last year? There have been some comments that he seemed different.'

Power nodded. 'Sometimes we had a game of squash and he didn't seem on form. When we went fishing, he was quieter than usual. He did come across as a bit flat at times, preoccupied. I thought it was to do with Lisa. With so many parties and socialising he found it hard when he had to get up for work. I asked him once if he was worried about anything but he just said yes, he was losing sleep over who would win the cup final. You know what blokes are like when they get together, they don't do heart-to-heart stuff.'

'You can leave that to us girls,' Louise told him. Power smiled down at her.

'Did Lisa work?'

'What didn't she do?' Power said. 'I saw her as a dabbler, never able to commit to anything. Dom didn't view it like that, naturally. He thought she was so talented she had to find different ways to express herself. To my knowledge, she'd been a model, a beautician, a jewellery seller, a restaurant greeter, and I think she ran a business with someone.'

'She thought she could sing,' Louise added with a hefty dose of spite. 'She fancied herself as a rock star. She told me she sang with some flaky group sometimes. Can't remember their name.'

'Were you invited to the party she held the night she died?'

They glanced at each other. Power coughed.

'Lisa did invite us but we decided not to go.'

'Her friends took quite a lot of drugs,' Louise added. 'After we'd been to one of those parties I said I didn't want to go to any more, with heaven knows what kind of goings on. Then I came down with flu anyway, so I was poorly sick.'

It seemed a middle-aged attitude for a woman of her age. He recalled DI Kharal mentioning vomit, semen and marijuana and reckoned Louise would definitely have disapproved of the "goings on" that night.

'Do you have any contacts you could give me for Lisa? I have her father's details.'

Power shrugged. 'We met her father at her funeral. He lives in Cape Town. As far as I know, she didn't have any family here. There was an ex-husband but I never met him. Her father said he would be coming back to deal with her flat and that if I wanted anything of Dom's to let him know. Other than that, we didn't move in her circles.'

'Georgie Merrell said that Lisa had a child.'

'Dom told me she had a daughter by the husband but I know nothing about her. She never referred to the child. Her father is your best bet.'

Louise had a tight smile, as if she begrudged giving it. 'I said to Mr Eastwood, if he decided to sell the flat I could market it for him.'

'You're an estate agent?'

'That's right. Granger and Siddons. Here's my card if you ever want advice property-wise.'

The card read *Louise Pullman, negotiator.* Clearly, a funeral was just another opportunity to tout for business as far as she was concerned. Power escorted him back downstairs and through the fish domain. He unlocked the door and stood with his hand on the handle.

'Ahm, just one more thing,' he said quietly. 'I didn't want to say this in front of Louise, she'd be annoyed. Dom asked me for a loan a couple of months before he died. He was strapped for cash and had some debt. Keeping up with Lisa was expensive. She liked to eat out and we're not talking pizza. And of course he had to pay Georgie.'

'How much did you lend him?'

'Five thousand.'

'Generous.'

'Maybe. I'm comfortably off. I made a lot of money on the markets before I bailed out to do what I'm really interested in.'

'Did he repay you?'

'No and I won't be looking to get it back. Water under the bridge. I just thought I should tell you in case it's of any significance. Don't mention it to Georgie, she's got enough to think about.'

Swift headed to the bus stop. The wind had dropped and the late afternoon was muggy. He unzipped his leather jacket and threw the Granger and Siddons card in a bin. He propped himself against a wall by the bus stop, listening to Bruce Springsteen through his earphones. Merrell and Lisa seemed an ill-matched couple in many ways, but differences could work in relationships. Merrell's words interested him: *There was a never-ending nightmare of blood and horror.* Why *never-ending*? It was an odd way of putting it, and the phrase circled in his head as he watched schoolchildren bicker and play fight on their way home.

CHAPTER 3

Swift was down at his rowing club, Tamesas, by seven a.m.
It was only ten minutes from his house to the river. When
the wind blew in the right direction, he could smell the
enticing, brackish aroma. He warmed up with some
stretches, and then checked his boat over before
launching. He sculled as far as Chiswick in fair conditions,
concentrating on his breathing and the trajectory of the
oars. The river was flowing fast and clean. He had brought
his binoculars in the hope of seeing a red-throated diver,
which made its winter home along this stretch of water.
There had been flooding in Chiswick when the river burst
its banks in February and he could see sandbags still
stacked against some of the high white houses and a
couple of the restaurants.

He paused to take a drink. The sky was a pale,
diffused rose. The breeze made a slight chop on the water
and nipped at his face. Some herring gulls screeched as a
low, laden barge thumped its way upstream. This was
where he was most at peace, where he found consolation.
His father had once told him a saying of Confucius: *a man
of wisdom delights in water.* Given the complications of his

life, Swift wasn't sure that he could claim much wisdom, but the delight was true and constant. He rubbed the scar on his thigh. He had sustained a deep knife wound while working with Interpol. Sometimes it pulled or ached when he exercised. He ran his thumbs along the ridged skin, watching a rabbit on the riverbank and thinking.

Mr Eastwood had replied to an email, saying he would be back in London in a couple of days and could meet him at his daughter's flat. Swift steered his boat in by the muddy river edge, took his phone out and looked up *Lisa Eastwood singing*. An item came up on YouTube for a band called Brainscan in the Nu Grunge category. He played the video which had been filmed unsteadily in what looked like a small club. There were three guitarists (two male, one female) and a male drummer, all wearing black T-shirts with a blue, pink and grey cross-section of a brain. Lisa stood out front in ripped grey jeans and the same T-shirt, like an urchin beauty. Her long curls flew wildly as she gyrated enthusiastically on the spot, stamping a booted foot, throwing her arms wide. Her voice was tuneful but not quite strong enough to hold up against the harsh guitars. The song was called *Hurt Moon* and had a fast, insistent pace. The sound quality was dull but some of the lyrics were audible:

> *You cut me like razors*
> *Never took my love*
> *Burned me, spurned me,*
> *Saw me on the ground*

He thought he wouldn't pay money to see them, although Lisa was stunning, her energy electrifying. He could see why Dominic Merrell would have found her a magnetic, captivating woman after eighteen steady, sober years as a family man. Why he had thrown caution to the winds was another question and one that only he could have answered.

Swift took up his oars and turned, feeling the tug of the tide as it started to flow in.

* * *

Swift was looking at a print of a grainy scan of a baby. Not his child but that of his cousin Mary and her partner, Simone. They had married the previous year and Simone was now pregnant with a boy, due a month after Ruth's. Swift and Mary had been close since childhood. She had helped him through the early death of his mother and he had supported her through some tribulations of her own. Both had gone into the Met and Mary was now an assistant commissioner. Swift found Simone difficult to get on with and therefore made an extra effort whenever he saw her. Mary loved her, so he just had to grit his teeth while he listened to Simone's insistent, extensive opinions on every topic of conversation. She had a painful talent for stating the obvious, and the thin-skinned person's flair for taking offence. The problem was that it was difficult these days to see Mary without Simone, who wanted to do everything with her partner and felt snubbed if not included in invitations. Swift missed the easy, meandering chats he used to have with Mary. A casual glass of wine in a bar, a stroll at Kew gardens or a lazy lunch with comfortable silences.

'Isn't he gorgeous?' Simone said, leaning across the restaurant table and pointing at the scan. 'Look at his darling toes! He seems to be doing yoga.'

Swift was aware of Mary's anxious glance, and knew she was concerned that he would be reminded of his own child. He nodded and handed the photo back to Simone.

'I'm glad everything is okay. You're looking so well.'

Simone was. Her skin was glowing and her maternity smock showed a high bump.

'I'm terrific. I've been watching my diet, taking small, regular meals, all well balanced. I monitor my fluid intake — at least eight glasses of water a day and no caffeine! I do special exercises, including swimming and slow walking. I've been writing a blog about it, dealing with each trimester, giving advice to other mums-to-be. Did you know?'

'I didn't.' He wasn't surprised.

'It's proved very popular, lots of comments and participation. You should tell Ruth, she might like to read it.'

'Simone . . .' Mary said softly, putting a hand on hers.

'Ty doesn't mind me mentioning Ruth, do you, Ty? I'm sure he's trying to be as involved as he can with his little one.'

He summoned a smile. 'I try, yes. Difficult at a distance, though.'

'I'm sure it will work out,' Simone said. 'Ruth clearly has feelings for you and after all, you do have rights as a father. I can't wait to hold our little cherub now. Oops, I must head for the Ladies. He's pressing somewhere he shouldn't!'

When Simone had disappeared, Mary looked at Swift and blew him a kiss. 'I'm sorry. She doesn't mean to be such a klutz.'

'It's okay. I don't need people to tiptoe around the subject of Ruth and the baby.' He took her hand and squeezed it. He loved her intelligent eyes, her brunette hair that reminded him of his mother and her warm laugh. Her presence reassured him.

'I know, but it can't be easy for you, seeing us and our pregnancy up close.'

'Sometimes it's an uncomfortable mirror image, but I just have to deal with that.'

'Have you heard from Ruth?' Mary asked.

'A couple of days ago.'

'Has she said where she is?'

'Only that she's staying with a friend in Devon. I have wanted to see her and talk to her but I didn't want to pressurise her. She was very fragile for a while when she found out about Emlyn's actions and his part in Kris's death. In the end, I had to accept that she needed to be on her own and concentrate on the baby. She is talking to Emlyn again.' Swift explained about Ruth's contact with her husband.

Mary chewed her lip. 'Oh. Not the best of news. That silver streak of hair at your temple is new. Looks distinguished, mind, amongst the black curls.'

He knew that Mary didn't have a high opinion of the turmoil Ruth had caused in his life. He touched his temple. 'It seemed to appear overnight. An outer sign of inner turmoil, I suppose. I have decided it's a badge of endurance. Cedric jokes that I'm catching up with him.'

'Considering what's happened, you're bearing up well.'

'I have to. I have an interesting new case. That helps distract me.' He told her about Merrell.

'What's your gut feeling?' she asked.

'I don't think he did it. Don't ask me why yet.'

'A difficult one, though, disproving a dead man's confession. Unless you can find someone else who admits to the killing.'

They poured more wine. Simone returned as the first course arrived, saying the trout looked great and Swift should remind Ruth to eat fish, but not swordfish or marlin as they were high in mercury. Suddenly, he'd had enough. He wanted to tell her to shut up. Instead, he started on his salmon, his appetite dwindling.

* * *

As he walked back home along the Thames path he saw Cedric emerge from their local pub, the Silver Mermaid. Beside him was a slight, slim figure, dark hair tied back with a ribbon. Cedric waved to him and beckoned him over.

'Ty! Good to see you. Did you enjoy your lunch?'

'I did. The expectant couple look well.' He glanced at the girl standing beside Cedric, recognising the Arsenal sweatshirt.

'Ty, this is Yana Ayo. The talented flute player by the kebab shop, you know.'

'Of course, yes. Hallo, Yana.' He held his hand out and she shook it fleetingly, looking down, then away.

'We had some lunch too. Fish and chips. Good, wasn't it, Yana?'

She nodded. 'Very good,' she said shyly. 'I must go now.'

'Won't you come back for a cup of tea?' Cedric asked.

'No, thank you. Thank you for my food.'

She darted away, head down, keeping away from the kerb.

'She was hungry. I had to tell her to eat slowly.' Cedric shook his head. 'I think she's sleeping rough.'

'How long has she been here?'

'It was difficult to get her to talk. I asked her about that bruise on her face and she said someone had punched her. I suppose she might be here illegally.'

'Maybe. It was good of you to buy her a meal.'

'It's not much. I wake up at night worrying about her. A girl like that, out on the streets and alone. I know there are many like her. It's just that I know her now, I know her name. It's personal.' For a moment, he looked older, frailer.

'We can both keep an eye on her when we're passing the kebab shop. Come on, I'll walk you home and make a cuppa.'

'The British answer to every worry.'

'Exactly.'

* * *

Harry Merrell was holding a green elastic band and was pinging it between his fingers. He was a solidly built, handsome young man, with strong forearms, the build of a rugby player. He had a surprisingly deep voice, his father's cleft chin and five silver earrings in his right ear lobe. His full beard was dense and he wore a close-fitting red and grey beanie hat. His T-shirt said, *Slave to the Rhythm*. He wore a black mourning band on his upper left arm, something Swift hadn't seen for a long time. Tension radiated from him, his jaw muscles worked silently. His brother Adam sat next to him on the sofa, hugging a Labrador puppy that now and again reached up and licked his chin. He had his mother's narrow frame and a startled expression, emphasised by his spiky hair and round glasses. Drumbeats had sounded from the garage next to their pebbledash, semi-detached house in Balham as Swift approached, and it had taken a while for Harry to appear, looking surly and reluctant.

Georgie Merrell had brought in coffee and fruit juice. The living room was comfortably furnished, with stacked bookshelves, magazines, sports trophies on the mantelpiece and a game of Monopoly on a low table by the bay window. The paraphernalia of family life. The chairs were covered with woven and quilted throws in bright colours and animal themes and there were striped rugs on the waxed floorboards. There were many framed photographs, and Dominic Merrell was in most of them. Georgie was maintaining the fiction that he had never left them. She was wearing a long, navy blue skirt and matching long-sleeved shirt with bell sleeves. She sat upright, her hair held back in a clip, her hands tucked into her sleeve ends and he was reminded again of a holy woman. Perhaps her integrity had proved too much for Merrell. It must have been hard to live up to.

The coffee was weak but fresh. When Georgie had finished dispensing the drinks, Swift nodded to the boys.

'I know your mum has explained why I've come round. I want to ask you a few things about your dad. If you feel upset at all, just say so, okay?'

Adam nodded, glancing at his mother. Harry carried on playing with his elastic, one leg hoisted across the knee of the other. He jiggled his foot, which seemed huge, in a blue and brown trainer with red laces. Best to start gently.

'What kinds of things did you do with your dad when he took you out?'

Adam spoke in a reedy voice. 'It depended on the weather really. If it wasn't that nice we went for a burger or bowling or to the cinema. Sometimes we played football. Just hung out at the park maybe.'

He glanced at Harry, then at his mother again. She smiled at him encouragingly. He stroked the puppy gently.

'Did you go to the flat where your dad lived with Lisa?'

'Yeah, sometimes.' Adam again. 'Sometimes we had tea there and watched TV or just mucked about. Well, not always Harry.'

Harry was spinning the elastic band on one finger. Nerves? Or an unwillingness to talk about his father.

'Did you stay over with him?'

Georgie spoke. 'There was only one bedroom there so it wasn't suitable. The boys always came home at night.'

'Right. Was Lisa there when you went back with your dad?'

Adam nodded. 'Not always, but some of the time. She liked to go out shopping. She laughed a lot but she couldn't cook. She tried macaroni cheese once and burnt it, set the smoke alarm off. The place used to be in a state. Dad did cleaning but he said it was hopeless cos Lisa and her mates just messed it up again.' The puppy pushed his nose into Adam's chest. 'Do you like our new puppy? He's called Sid. His colour's fox red.'

Swift didn't care for dogs. 'He's very handsome. When did you get him?'

'Three weeks ago. Dad liked dogs but he couldn't have one cos they weren't allowed where he lived.'

Harry made a grunting noise and wound the elastic around his wrist.

Swift spoke more sharply. 'Harry, did you get on with Lisa?'

The boy shifted on the sofa. 'Yeah. She was okay I s'pose.'

Swift had an urge to reach out and still the jiggling foot. 'I know it can't have been easy for you. You can feel divided loyalties in that kind of situation.'

Harry cast him a baleful glance. 'You a shrink as well as a detective, then?'

'Harry!' his mother said. 'There's no need to be rude.'

'That's okay,' Swift said mildly. At least he had a response and some fleeting eye contact. 'I think in a way you do have to be a bit of a shrink when you're a detective. You have to try and read people, especially if you think they might be lying to you.' He was taking a gamble, hoping Georgie wouldn't be offended. 'That way you've been playing with the elastic band for example, Harry. It could be read as distress or as a way of distracting you from the subject of your dad.'

Harry sniffed but his foot stopped moving. The puppy put a paw on his arm and he pushed it away roughly.

'Did your dad seem sad at all recently?'

There was a long pause.

'You know a bit down, upset,' Swift added.

'Don't think so,' Adam said. 'He must have been sad, though. He didn't say.' He put his face into the puppy's neck.

Georgie leaned forward and patted his knee.

'Harry, did you notice anything unusual about your dad?'

'Nope.'

'Right. Had you heard him and Lisa arguing at all?'

Harry shrugged.

Adam looked up. 'They never argued. They were always, you know, hugging and stuff.'

Georgie closed her eyes. Swift felt as if he were wading through treacle. The puppy sighed and he thought *me too*.

'This is hard, I know. Did your dad contact either of you in the days after Lisa died and before he died?'

They both shook their heads.

'I am trying to understand what happened with your dad and because I never knew him, anything you think is important might help me. Did you know Lisa sang with a band?'

Adam nodded. Harry's foot jittered frantically.

'How about you, Harry? You look as if you knew. You could loosen up a bit, help me out here. Not talking is sort of selfish and it's hard on your younger brother.'

Harry flicked the elastic band across the room and stood up abruptly, knocking a cushion off the sofa. He stood with his hands in fists. Spittle flew through the air as he spoke but his soft brown eyes held deep pain.

'It's all done, all over and nothing can bring him back. He killed himself, end of. I don't need you giving me advice or asking me fucking stupid questions, and I don't want a fucking stinky puppy as a replacement for my father, either.' He barged out of the room, banging the door behind him.

'Adam, can you take Sid out in the garden for a bit?' Georgie nodded to her son and he carried the dog away.

She sank back in the chair. 'Sorry,' she said. 'They've both been upset but Harry has been really moody and difficult. He's been that way for a while, but now . . . he even snarls at Adam and that's unfair.' Drums started banging, the wall vibrated. 'He spends all his time in the garage, playing his drums or at friends' houses.'

'It's hard for him, and your husband's death is fraught in so many ways.'

'Yes. I'm glad you understand.' She looked worn, her skin translucent in the fading afternoon light.

'Have you any family who can help you?'

'My mother is dead. I have a father and brother in Carlisle but that's a long way away and I can't expect them to be at my beck and call. I am trying to keep things as normal as possible, but of course nothing is. We're the walking wounded, limping along. I get so utterly exhausted. I'd like to sleep for a year.'

Swift nodded, thinking sleep was unlikely with Harry's constant racket. A phone rang and she excused herself, saying it might be about work. Swift heard her go upstairs. He waited a moment, then walked through the trim house past the kitchen and stepped into the long, rectangular garden where Adam was throwing a rubber bone for Sid. The afternoon sun drew blades of light and shade across the grass. There was a boot scraper by the back door and flower borders framing the deep green lawn, bursting with orange and scarlet tulips and clumps of white snowdrop anemones. A cherry tree stood at the far end, heavy with pale pink flowers. Beside it was a shed painted sea blue. The house and the garden spoke of careful tending, of being cherished. The dog was running around dementedly on the damp grass. Adam was laughing, his cheeks flushed.

'That looks like good fun,' Swift said.

Adam smiled. 'He loves it. Mum says he's like a toddler, it's good to tire him out.'

'And you get tired out too!'

Swift saw the sense in Georgie's dog therapy. He watched the game while Adam chatted on about Sid and the mischief he got up to. The boy and the dog were panting. He was glad that Georgie had her younger son to distract her and keep her sane. He felt a twinge of guilt at pumping the guileless Adam for information but didn't let it stop him.

He said casually, 'Harry seemed to get a bit upset when I mentioned Lisa singing with a band.'

Adam stroked the puppy's ears as it jumped up at him. 'Yeah. He was fed up cos she said she could get him some drum gigs with them but she didn't come through on it. He said she was a fake.'

'Was this recently?'

'Think so. No, Sid, don't slobber on me, that's yuk! I'm going to take him to obedience classes when he's a bit older so that he's trained properly.'

'Sounds a good idea. I'm glad you had some good times with your dad and Lisa, some laughs, even if Harry didn't always join you.'

'Yeah. It was better when Harry didn't come. It was easier. Harry's moody. Sometimes he'd join in, other times he'd sit and refuse to talk. Mum says it's his age. Dad said that too. Lisa said that she was a nightmare when she was a teenager.'

'Well, growing up can be hard. I think it's going to rain. I had better head off.'

More photos lined the hallway and he stopped to look at them. They were mostly family shots of the four of them, taken when the boys were younger. Harry smiling, before the adolescent hormones and turmoil kicked in. There was a large one of the Merrells' wedding with Georgie's parents at her side, Dominic's at his. Swift examined it. Something about it bothered him. He stood closer but the nudge of unease was no clearer. Georgie Merrell appeared on the landing, holding her phone and talking about portrait sizes. Swift waved goodbye and she nodded.

As he left the house, he saw that the garage was open. Harry was leaning against the door, smoking and drumming his fingers against the wall. He looked away as Swift zipped his jacket up.

'Your brother tells me that Lisa said she was going to get you drum gigs with Brainscan. You didn't mention that earlier.'

He blew an expert smoke ring, studying it as it spiralled up. 'Why should I?'

'It means you knew her rather better than you were letting on. Did she get you any gigs?

'No.'

'Weren't you good enough?'

Harry coloured. 'It didn't work out, that's all.'

'Still, you must have been disappointed. Did she let you down? I get the impression she took life pretty lightly.'

'What do you know?' Harry took a last drag and threw the cigarette butt on the ground. He ground it hard with his heel.

'If I don't ask, I don't get.' Swift moved around him, gesturing at the gleaming white scooter with red leather saddle in the garage. 'Nice bike. Vespa 946. Not cheap. Is that the one your dad bought you?'

'Yeah.'

'You're eighteen. Are you still at school?'

'Yeah. Now piss off.'

He stepped back and slammed the garage door shut. Swift waited for a few minutes, feeling the first raindrops fall, listening to the angry drums start up again. *Thudthudthud*. Harry Merrell's emotions became remarkably raw whenever the enchanting, flirty Lisa was mentioned.

* * *

Ruth rang him while he was on the train to West Dulwich, heading to see Lisa's father. It was months since he had heard her husky voice. He felt a joy that he had missed keenly but fought it down, knowing it could be treacherous.

'Is this a good time?' she asked.

'It's okay. I'm on my way to an appointment.'

'I'm sorry it's taken so long for this, for me to phone you. I've just been so confused . . .'

'You're here now.'

'Can we meet? Either in Brighton or I could come to you.'

'Brighton? Does that mean you're back with Emlyn?'

'I'd rather talk to you in person, Ty. Please.'

The train slowed at a signal. He watched a man working on a roof, cementing a chimney pot.

'I'd prefer London, then. Come to my place. I don't want to talk in a restaurant, in public.'

'No, of course. Can you email me with some dates you can do?'

'I'll send them later today. You're well, and the baby?'

'Fine, everything is fine.'

Hardly, he thought, saying goodbye. It was drizzling, the rain streaking furrows through the grimy train windows. The carriage smelled of socks and vomit and tinny music was leaking through the earphones of a woman near him. The address he was heading to, near Dulwich Park, wasn't far from where he and Ruth had lived when they were engaged. He had returned there one evening from working in Lyon to find her waiting with the news that she was leaving him. More than six years ago and he could still feel the tremors of the shock as if it had been yesterday. She had run off and married Emlyn and yet here they were now, inextricably bound together by a child. She was as familiar and dear to him as she had always been. He knew the scent of her skin, the food and music she liked, her habits and mannerisms, the way she danced her fingers through the air when she laughed. He knew everything there was to know about her and he knew nothing.

CHAPTER 4

The train idled into West Dulwich and gave an exhausted sigh of brakes. He pulled up the collar of his jacket and walked fast through the rain. The flat where Lisa and Merrell had lived was on the third floor of a three storey thirties built block, fronting the park. He was buzzed in through an intercom and ascended curving stairs with an oak banister. Donald Eastwood was standing in the open doorway of the flat, a bottle of beer in his hand.

'Come on in, Mr Swift.' He waved the bottle. 'Clearing up is thirsty work. Want one of these?'

Swift accepted, following him down a wide hallway with art deco mirrors and lights, into a bright living room. It was filled with cardboard boxes, sheets of newspaper, bubble wrap, rolls of sticky tape and brimming black rubbish bags. Lighter squares on the pale cream walls showed where pictures had been removed. The blinds were pulled up, revealing the beauty of the rectangular art deco windows with geometric design panels. The park opposite looked woebegone in the rain, the tall ranks of plane trees still bare after winter.

Eastwood opened a beer and handed it to him. He was a thickset, suntanned man, leathery-skinned with a light brown thatch of hair that looked like a toupee. He had a pendulous beer gut and wattles on his neck. Once handsome, probably athletic, but gone to seed. His accent was South African, his voice a throaty rumble.

'There's an armchair for you. I'll pull up this dining chair.'

Swift sat on the black leather chair. The décor and integrated white wood cabinets were grubby and he could see that the fawn carpet was dirt-marked and worn. There was no sofa and he assumed that Eastwood must have got rid of it and its bloodstains. The beer was cold and refreshing and he was glad of it after the unexpected call from Ruth.

'Thanks for seeing me. Please accept my condolences.'

'Yah. Not the news a father wants or expects. My only child, you see.'

'I didn't know that.'

'Yah. My little girl. I set her up in life, bought her this flat. She had to come to London. That was her dream, so I went along with her. Some dream now. A nightmare.' He gestured around. 'Never thought I'd have to do this, clear out her life. I've made a start in here, but there's loads to do. Find myself stopping, looking at something of hers, and choking up. Y'know?'

'It must be very hard. When did Lisa move to London?'

'When she was twenty, ten years ago. She got work modelling. Some agency or other.'

'I'd like to find out a bit more about your daughter from you. Dominic Merrell's wife can't believe he murdered her. There is no motive or reason why he claimed to have done it.'

'Yah, well . . . I dunno. I never met the guy. Lisa said he was sweet, good to her. A true romantic, she reckoned.

Took her to Capri for her thirtieth birthday last October, booked a luxury hotel.'

Eastwood took a deep slug of beer, rocking slightly on his chair. Swift wondered how many he had already downed, and wondered also if Finbar Power's loan had been needed to pay for the fancy holiday.

'Did Lisa say anything to you about arguing with Merrell or any problems they had?'

'Nah. As far as I knew, everything was hunky dory.'

'I understand Lisa had been married. Can you tell me about that?'

'Yah, she married a guy called JoJo Hayworth. Still was married, they never got round to divorcing. He's a model, that's how they met. I came for the wedding, paid for it. He seemed an okay guy, a good looker. Bit full of himself but they seemed well matched. They had a kid but they only lasted two years. She had a big heart, did Lisa. She loved too easily, gave her heart too easily. I think she gave him money to get rid of him but she kept this flat in her name, thank goodness.'

'Where are her husband and child now?'

'JoJo's around somewhere, don't know where he lives. I can give you his number. The kid, Tamsin, lives with JoJo's mother in Canterbury. I'm going to see her before I fly back.'

'Was there a reason why Tamsin didn't live with your daughter?'

'Her work, is what she told me. She was still doing some modelling after Tamsin was born and she had late hours. JoJo's mum offered to do the childcare and Canterbury is not that far from London. Lisa spent a lot of time with her own gran back in Cape Town after I divorced, so I guess she knew it would work okay.'

That sounded flimsy. Swift imagined that Lisa had fed her doting father filtered information. 'Did she have other boyfriends you knew about, before Dominic?'

'Well, y'know, I'm over in Cape Town. We talked now and again by phone. She mentioned a couple of fellas she liked well enough. There was a Richard and a Perry. I think one of them lived here for a while.'

'Had Lisa always lived here?'

'Yah, I bought this for her for when she moved to London. Worth a small fortune now.' His eyes watered. 'The police believed Dominic killed her. I don't understand it either. Took away my beautiful Lisa. Maybe he got angry because of the abortion, I don't know.'

'She'd had an abortion?'

'Yah. That's what the police told me. Post-mortem showed she'd had a recent abortion. She didn't mention it to me so I don't know what happened there. I guess they didn't want any more children.' He took a large monogrammed hanky from a pocket and passed it across his eyes. 'Another beer?'

'No thanks, I'm fine. Do you know if anyone else knew about the termination?' Kharal had left out that detail.

'No idea.' He finished his beer and burped softly. 'It's hard, doing this on my own, y'know?'

'Lisa's mother isn't around?'

'Nah. We divorced ages ago. She went back to Peru, remarried, lost touch with both of us. She was a model too when I met her. A real beauty. Lisa got her looks. Oh, y'know, she was just a lovely, lovely girl, Mr Swift. Always smiling and laughing. Such a generous heart and a sweet nature. She wouldn't have harmed a fly.'

Swift put his empty beer bottle in one of the bin bags. Maybe, but she seemed to cause havoc while she was doing all that smiling and laughing. He chose his words carefully for this doting, bereaved father.

'I get a picture of your daughter as a very sociable, fun-loving woman.'

'Oh yah. She loved to party and she was the life and soul. She had this zest for life, right from when she was a baby. Everyone loved her. Burned the candle at both ends, did Lisa,' he said proudly.

'She did other jobs besides modelling?'

'That's right. She liked to branch out, try her hand at new things.' He smiled. 'When she was at school one of her teachers said in a report that she *could charm gold from a miser.* That was my Lisa! She owned a business with a friend, too, an Isabella Alfaro. That's what she was concentrating on in the last couple of years.'

'Do you know the name of the business?'

'Oh yah. I gave her money to help set it up. I was glad she wanted to build something. She owned a major share and I'm what's called a silent partner. It's called Body Balm. I think the turnover's been reasonable. I left it to the girls to get on with. It's a holistic therapy thing. Y'know, massage and stuff. It's based on a boat on the river. Somewhere near King's Cross.'

He meant the Regent's Canal. 'It sounds as if Lisa was okay financially, as well as owning this flat.'

'I guess. I mean, she always seemed okay. I told her last year I wouldn't be able to give her any more money for a good while. My business back home is all right but not booming. I'm watching the balance sheet.'

Eastwood's phone rang. He checked the caller ID and said he needed to take it. Swift asked if it was okay to have a look around and he nodded, moving to the window.

Along the hallway from the living room was a small utility room with a washing machine and tumble dryer. It smelled of mildew and the floor tiles were torn. An ironing board was propped against the wall. The next room was the bathroom, equipped with walk-in shower, bidet and two hand basins. The tiles were streaked and grimy and one of the basins had a large crack down one side. Swift looked in the cabinet. The shelves wore a jumble of sleeping tablets, aspirin, toothpaste tubes, combs and brushes, lipsticks, hair sprays, dental floss and bottles of moisturiser. Two dead plants stood on the window ledge beside more cans of hair mousse, razors, cleansers, gels and skin creams. The names on all the products were high end, nothing from a supermarket. He moved on to the kitchen which was in a similar state of disarray, full of gadgets which would once have been gleaming but were now dulled with grease and dust. The cooker was filthy, the white cupboard doors showing finger marks. The quartz-tiled floor was sticky beneath his feet. At the end of the hallway was a large bedroom with a wide bed, deep green carpet, built-in light oak wardrobes on either side of the bed and a dressing table littered with cosmetics, perfumes, cotton wool, hairdryer and curling tongs and packets of painkillers. A couple of lacy coffee-coloured bras hung from the corner of the mucky mirror. He opened the wardrobes on the right and saw crammed rows of Lisa's clothes and stacks of shoes. Her bedside table held a Jackie Collins novel, a glass of water, a couple of miniature whiskies and a small photo of a little girl on a swing. The drawers and wardrobes to the left of the bed were empty. Merrell had been cleared away.

He stood by the window and looked about him. The carpet was in need of a vacuum and every surface was dusty. He guessed that the flat had been in mint condition when Lisa moved in and she had done no maintenance. The place told him nothing except that the owner cared little about her environment. Regular crowded parties would have caused considerable wear and tear. Adam had been right about his father and stepmother's domestic life.

He went back to the living room as Eastwood finished his call.

'Sorry about that. My housckccper needing instructions.'

'That's okay. I wondered, did Lisa leave a will?'

'Don't think so. I haven't found one. I was always telling her she should make one but y'know, she was young, she thought death was a long way down the road if she thought of it at all.'

'So JoJo Hayworth will benefit nicely.'

'Yah. I spoke to a solicitor and she explained the rules of intestacy. As the widower, JoJo gets Lisa's possessions, £250K from the sale of this property and half of the rest of her estate. It grates but I guess that's how Lisa wanted it. JoJo emailed me to say he didn't want any of her things and to take what I liked so I'm just going through. I'd like little Tamsin to have a few keepsakes. He can deal with the rest. I suppose I should have been wiser and put my name on the deeds but there you go.'

He seemed to have a laid-back attitude to money, Swift thought, and had passed it on to his daughter. He watched as Eastwood reached into one of the boxes and took out a framed photo, rubbing the glass with his sleeve.

'Here, this is when she was modelling. Wasn't she just so beautiful?'

Swift took the photo. Lisa was in a diaphanous black and silver lace top that ended under the bust, partnered with a calf-length black skirt trimmed with the same silver. She wore hooped silver earrings. Her head was thrown a little to one side, her eyes and teeth gleaming as she beamed at the camera. The photo spoke of vitality, poise and of course, great beauty.

'She was very lovely,' he said. 'When do you go back to Cape Town?'

'End of the week. I have the business to run, pet foods, can't be away too long.'

'Is it okay to email you if I need to ask anything else?'

'Sure, yah. If someone else did do this to my little girl, I hope you find him. I'd offer a reward if you think it would help.'

'I wouldn't advise that for now. A reward can cause all kinds of activity that just clouds matters. Let me carry on with asking questions for now.'

'Okay. I just can't think why anyone would harm my Lisa, especially a guy who loved her. It would be hard to find a more genuine heart in the whole of this great city.' He looked away, his eyes glassy.

Eastwood's trusting take on his daughter was understandable, if a little naïve. Swift supposed that the long distance adult relationship meant that his Lisa was always the blameless, charming little girl he had known years ago. He took contact details for Mrs Hayworth in Canterbury and for Isabella Alfaro. He left Eastwood to his sorting and packing, another beer in his hand.

As he headed for the stairs Swift stepped back to allow a dapper-looking man to come up. He was holding two heavy shopping bags in one hand and finishing a phone conversation. Swift nodded and waited until he had said *ciao* several times.

'Were you a neighbour of Ms Eastwood?' he asked.

'That's right. I'm next door. Who are you? Are you clearing her flat?'

'No, I'm a private detective, looking into her murder. I came to speak to her father.'

'Oh yeah, poor guy.' He put his shopping down. He was small and sallow-skinned with a petulant mouth.

'Did you know Ms Eastwood?'

'Only to complain to her.'

'About what?'

'Noise. Parties. Music. Singing. More noise. More parties that went on until five or six in the morning. People tramping up and down the stairs, hallway stinking of cigarette smoke and other substances, cigarette butts thrown in the front garden. Get the picture?'

'Vividly. How did she respond to your complaints?'

'Lisa? What can I say? She'd smile,' he put his head to one side and mimicked a sweet look, 'say of course, of course, she was so, so sorry, it wouldn't happen again. Then it did. She thought because she was beautiful and invited me to her parties and left bottles of expensive champagne outside my door, that made it all okay.' He was warming to his theme, leaning against the wall, arms

57

folded. 'I told her that I had to work and I didn't appreciate shouting and laughing and bloody awful music at all hours. I am sorry she was murdered, that was dreadful, but I'm glad she has gone from the building. I was at my wits' end with her.'

'I can imagine. What about her partner, Dominic?'

'I spoke to him once. Sweet guy, quiet, unlike her. Very civil and apologetic but I don't think he had much say about what went on. Looked like a rabbit caught in the headlights when he was around her. He did it, didn't he? That came as a surprise, I wouldn't have thought he could cut butter but I guess the worm turned.'

'Did you meet any of the people she entertained?'

'No. I didn't attend any of the parties. I saw some of them on the stairs occasionally. Most of them looked around her age or younger, all ripped jeans and messy hair and T-shirts, you know. That night she died, I stayed at a friend's place because I knew there was another party planned. One of the other neighbours said the place was heaving. As I said, I didn't really know Lisa except as a major headache. If you want to know more about her, you should talk to Malory Meredith on the ground floor, number three. They were pals.'

Swift thanked him, ran downstairs and rang the bell of number three. There was no reply. He wrote on one of his cards, asking Ms Meredith to phone him, and put it through her letterbox.

He had not planned to go to the café where he and Ruth used to eat Sunday brunch, always the same meal — scrambled eggs with smoked salmon. But he found himself in there, ordering a plate of hummus and olives with flat breads. It had changed hands and now specialised in smoothies. There was a long list of flavours on a blackboard above the counter, including ingredients he had never tasted, chia seeds and goji for example. He chose a goji berry and mango smoothie to go with his food, found a table and watched the rain tumble and run along the gutters. It was only mid-afternoon but the light was dim and misty. He yawned, feeling lethargic, a headache growing behind his eyes. The smoothie did not impress him. He pushed it aside and ordered a coffee, waiting for the caffeine to kick in. Money from a property in Dulwich and proceeds from a business. JoJo Hayworth was going to benefit rather nicely from his wife's death, and people had killed for less. Had he known there was no will? He rang Hayworth and the number in Canterbury and left messages, then googled Body Balm and found the website. It told him that he could visit a canal boat *where your cares and stresses will be soothed away on a charming waterway in the heart of London*. He phoned the number and waited for an answer. He watched a man on the pavement conducting a silent mime as he struggled unsuccessfully with a broken umbrella before dumping it in a bin and hurrying away.

* * *

Winter was clinging on. Earlier in the day, there had been vivid razor slashes of lightning and ominous rolling thunder. The rain had persisted for a week, mixed at times with sleet and hail. The trees looked tattered. The narcissi, primroses and hellebores Lily had planted in the back garden were bedraggled.

Swift sat with Ruth in the hazy light of late afternoon. Her head was on his shoulder, her hand in his. He'd had a shock when he opened the door. Her long butterscotch hair had gone, replaced with a short, feathery cut. She told him she had needed to do something radical. Time to leave behind that other Ruth and face the future. It made her look younger and more vulnerable, her face pared down.

At first, they had both been nervous, like polite acquaintances, eating the lunch he had prepared, even talking about the weather. But then she had leaned across, taken his hand and placed it on her abdomen. He felt the baby kick and laughed and the ice was broken.

She had agreed to go back to Emlyn, give the marriage another chance.

'In the end, I am his wife. I made promises to him. He is terribly ill and he needs me. It's heart breaking to see a man who was so active and brilliant brought so low. Ty, he deeply regrets, we both deeply regret what happened. Emlyn is so ashamed and ridden with guilt. He has written you a letter. I brought it with me.'

'What about the angry rages he used to fly into? How are you going to cope with those again?'

'He says they've gone, burned away, and I believe him. He never used to be like that, you know. It's part of MS for some people, but it doesn't necessarily last. He is a frail, sickly, shadow of a man, Ty. He's being slowly destroyed.' She turned and touched his whitened temple. 'Did you love Kris?'

'No, not love. But I think I might have in time.'

Love with Ruth had been immediate, overwhelming and rapturous. A *coup de foudre*. They had looked at each other across a table in the café of the British Museum and they had *known*. He doubted you could have that twice in a life.

She sighed. 'I love you still. I always have but I was careless and I lost track of the love. I do love Emlyn but I've never been able to forget you. I can't explain it to myself. Perhaps it's inexplicable. I wish I could stop loving you because it would be better for you, but I can't.'

'I know,' he said. 'It's just how it is. It's how it has always been.'

There was a silence. He had lit a fire, a rare event, and the soft hiss of the wood was cheering.

'This is a lovely room,' Ruth said. 'It's got a sense of harmony. I'm so fond of that William Morris wallpaper, even though it's faded in places.'

Swift nodded, looking around. The square, well-proportioned room was almost exactly as it had been when his aunt was alive. It was furnished simply in the Arts and

Crafts style with a Victorian chaise longue and deep armchairs in a thistle-patterned fabric. The elm floor was covered with dark red rugs. It was comfortable and peaceful, facing north east, so always slightly shaded, a refuge when needed.

'You mean this room suits me, a bit shabby and past its best?'

She laughed. 'It may be a little tattered but it has character. It's been here a long time and it knows it has stood the test of the years.'

'Aunt Lily would like to hear that. She was a woman who saw no point in change for change's sake and I suppose I resemble her in that way.'

He moved away and hunkered down to feed the fire with another block of wood. Orange flames leaped, and then settled. He spoke without turning.

'How am I going to see our child, Ruth? I don't want to come to your house in Brighton and pretend to be at ease with Emlyn.'

'What if he went out? His carer takes him places and . . .'

'No,' He stood and looked at her. 'Don't ask that of me. I don't want to see my daughter in your marital home.'

'Okay. I understand. Look, Ty, I don't have the answer but we can work something out. I will come to London if need be. Emlyn wants you to see as much of the baby as you like.'

'Generous of him.'

She reached for her bag. 'Will you read this letter now, please? I'd rather you did while I'm here.'

'Have you read it?'

'Yes. I typed it for Emlyn. He finds it hard work to control a pen or keyboard now. I'm going to the bathroom.'

He sat on the carpet by the fire, his back against an armchair and read:

Tyrone,

I can only say that I am deeply sorry for my actions last year and the pain and grief they caused you. I am not going to blame my illness but I do believe that it made me mentally unstable for some time. The death of Kris Jelen will always haunt me. I'm not asking you to forgive me but I hope that for the sake of the baby, you can tolerate my presence in her life. I hope that we can just do our best for her.

Emlyn Williams.

He held the letter for a moment, an angry panic flooding through him as he recalled finding Kris's body on the floor of her living room. Her parents had flown from Poland, and he saw again their anguished faces, sitting dazed and distraught in a shabby police station. He had never seen Lodz, where Kris was born and grew up. There had been no time to get to know the country and culture she came from, but she had become dear to him and her death was burned on his conscience. Emlyn Williams's words were humble and filled with regret but a talented young life had been ended because of his rage and jealousy. He crumpled the paper and threw it in the fire. He watched it flare and dissolve in flames. Burning as cleansing. Maybe. Like Ruth, he did not have the answer.

She returned and sat, wriggling against the sofa to get comfortable, pulling a cushion behind her back. She had always been so slim and fleet. He was still adjusting to this pregnant woman who moved more slowly.

'I've read the letter and burned it. I don't doubt his remorse but I can't forgive him. Let's work out what we can.' He sat beside her, touching her hand. 'A woman recently described her family to me as the walking wounded. It resonated with me. Are you tired or would you like a walk by the river, despite the rain?'

'I'd love it. Just a little walk, though. I have to pace myself.'

That reminded him of Simone's blog and he told her about it as they left the house under the shelter of a huge umbrella. She laughed, placing a hand over the bump in her coat. They turned down to the river, backs to the wind.

'What are Mary and Simone going to call their baby?'

'They haven't decided yet. I think they've narrowed it down to a list of six.'

'I've thought of a name for our daughter. I think, I hope, you'll like it.'

'Yes?'

She stopped and looked out at the river. It was dark and rushing, the wind scouring it. The lozenges of amber light on the pavement illuminated the flashing raindrops.

'I'd like to call her Branna. And your surname, so Branna Swift. What do you think?'

His mother's name. 'Thank you. That's a lovely thought, a lovely name.'

She nodded. 'I think I've had enough now. Do you know what I'd really like to do?'

'What?'

'Go back and use the toasting fork to make toast at the fire. Do you have white bread? It has to be white.'

'We can call at the corner shop. They always have sliced white. We can have it with Cedric's gooseberry jam from last summer.'

'It would be lovely to see him. Is he in?'

'I told him you were coming. I'll knock on his door.'

* * *

Ruth sat on a small tapestry covered stool in front of the fire and started on the toast while he switched on lamps, drew the curtains against the drenched world, put the kettle on and fetched Cedric.

'Ah, the fire is just right,' Cedric said, kissing Ruth. 'Lily used to make toast like this every evening in the winter. Sometimes we had it with salmon paste or honey or best of all, golden syrup!'

They sat on either side of Ruth, mugs of tea poured, covering the warm, browned slices with their charred edges with butter and thick dollops of deep red jam. There was a glow on her face as she speared another piece of bread and held it to the grate, saying that since being pregnant, she craved the carbonised flavour and texture of crisp, burnt food. Hail rattled against the windows and wind moaned in the chimney. The lamps shed a soft circle of buttery light. Swift experienced a moment of pure childlike happiness, a brief illusion that he and Ruth had never parted, that darkness was held at bay and all was right with the world.

There was a noise from upstairs, the sound of someone moving around.

'Is Oliver with you?' Swift asked Cedric.

His friend looked shifty. 'No. I met Yana. I let her have a bath and she fell asleep on my sofa. She was on the street, wet through and exhausted. I've dried her things out for her.' He turned to Ruth. 'Yana is a refugee, from Syria. She is seventeen and homeless.'

'How sad,' Ruth said. 'Would she like some toast?'

'Better not just now,' Cedric said. 'She's very shy and it took all my persuasive powers to get her to come home with me to dry out. I'll go up and check on her, make her a sandwich before she goes. Lovely to see you, Ruth, and of course the baby too.'

Ruth left in a taxi soon after, waving to him from the misted window. Swift cleared up and selected Joe Cocker from his playlist. He poured a glass of red wine and sat in front of the fading fire. Cocker started singing *The Simple Things*, one of his mother's favourite songs. Whenever she heard it, she would dance and wax lyrical about the time she had seen him in concert. Swift lifted his drink in a silent toast to the departed, and the expected, Branna.

He picked over the reality of Ruth moving back to her husband. Not for the first time, he entertained uncomfortable thoughts about Williams and how long the man might live. He had looked up the prognosis for MS. It was not a fatal illness but Williams had a rare and progressive form of it. He was already in a wheelchair and experienced difficulties swallowing and with speech and had a tremor in his hands. Early death could happen through infection or pneumonia. Am I hoping for this man's speedy demise, willing it almost? He asked himself the question and couldn't deny that the idea had its attractions. Williams had wrought havoc in his life and brought him terrible grief, taking away two women dear to him. He felt an icy dislike of himself, for thinking such things. And then what? Ruth and their daughter would come and live with him and all would be well? Hardly. She loved him still and he loved her. It was the simplest thing in the world. It was the most complicated.

He put a last log on the dormant fire, poked it into life and lay on the rug in front of it, staring into the lambent golden flames until they flickered and fell into soft grey ash.

CHAPTER 5

Swift answered his phone as he walked along the busy towpath by the Regent's canal. Spring had decided to shoulder its way in overnight and a sudden warm sun had left everyone looking happily stunned. The caller announced that he was Stewart Turner, manager of the Hays hotel in Barnet.

'I was talking to Dora Madibe at one of our network meetings,' he said. 'She told me about your contact with her and your investigation. I thought I should ring you. I feel so sorry for the Merrell family.'

'Okay. Did Dominic Merrell work at your hotel too?'

'That's right. That's why I'm calling you.' He cleared his throat. 'Look, this is a bit delicate. I wouldn't want you repeating information. It's just that — well, I liked the bloke and if he didn't kill that woman and this might help you in any way . . .'

'Okay. Whatever you tell me will be confidential.'

'Not long before he . . . well, before he died, I had to speak to Merrell. There had been some petty thefts in the hotel, from staff, not guests. A tenner here, twenty there, that kind of thing. One of those situations where people couldn't be absolutely sure they hadn't lost the money but it was happening too frequently to be accidental. As you can imagine, we get a lot of this in the hotel business. I thought it was probably one of the employees so I was keeping an eye open before I reported it officially. I walked into the staff area and found Merrell looking in someone's bag. I took him to my office and challenged him about it and he confirmed he was the thief. He broke down. It was quite disturbing.'

'How much are we talking in total?'

'About fifty pounds or so at our hotel.'

'What did he say about it?'

'That he'd had a lot of turmoil in his personal life, was in financial trouble and had debts. He was so apologetic and upset . . . it was the toughest conversation I've ever had with a member of staff. He begged me to let him pay it back and not to report him to the police. I knew he had worked for the company for a long time and was well regarded. I said I'd have to consult my management.'

Swift knew that the first time someone was caught stealing was rarely the first time they'd done it. 'You're about to tell me he was taking money elsewhere.'

'Correct. I contacted the other managers and one of them reported similar problems. There were none at the Southwark branch, so Dora wasn't involved.'

'Any idea how much money he had taken overall?'

'It was just over three hundred. I spoke to our regional director and she took advice. She came back and said that given Dominic's long service with the company and the small amount stolen, she wouldn't contact the police but we would have to let him go. She was about to contact him when he hanged himself and we decided not to take any further action after he died. His family had enough to worry about. We recompensed the staff for their losses and left it at that.'

'That was a decent move. Thanks a lot for letting me know. I won't pass on the information to anyone.'

He stood for a moment, watching a green-and-red canal boat move slowly along the water. A girl was doing yoga in the cabin, the warrior pose. He was glad that Merrell's family didn't have to add him being a thief to their list of woes. A man would hardly hang himself over petty theft, unless it was just the last burden in a mounting series of troubles. Perhaps Merrell had borrowed and stolen money from a number of sources and had massive debts. There was the five thousand he had borrowed from Finbar Power and would want to repay. He must have expected his employer to take the theft seriously. He might have anticipated dismissal from his job and the possibility of police involvement. The future would have looked bleak. No more holidays in Capri, and he would have to face his family. Feelings of shame and embarrassment could explain suicide but did not suggest a motive for stabbing Lisa. A tipping point maybe. He might have discovered she was seeing another man. Perhaps she had the abortion because the child was someone else's. He might have told her that he was in financial trouble and likely to lose his job and her response had been disparaging. Swift knew of murderers who had claimed that the act was the accumulation of years of arguments and bad feeling. He recalled a man who said he had beaten his wife to death because she nagged him constantly, and he finally flipped when she criticised the way he had made the bed. Yet nobody so far had mentioned that Merrell and Lisa had ever been at odds. On the contrary, he had seemed devoted to her.

He walked on past a terraced area where people were sitting, faces raised to the sun and stopped to browse at a floating bookshop where he bought a couple of novels and a slim paperback with photos of the Thames. A little further on was a boat selling artisan breads and herbs. The herbs festooned the deck in pots: marjoram, parsley, several types of mint, oregano, basil, rosemary, borage, chervil, chives, dill and lemon balm. The air smelled heady with their fragrance. He selected pots of lemon balm and spearmint for Cedric, who loved to use fresh herbs in his cooking and a loaf of caraway seed bread for himself. He carried on past a houseboat selling multi-coloured scarves, tie-dyed dresses and crocheted capes and came to Body Balm, which was on a boat called Aurora Dawn, painted yellow and cream. Pansies and geraniums made a colourful display in painted metal containers along the sides. The front deck area had a dark green awning and several striped canvas chairs. Music was playing quietly, the sound of tinkling bells. He stepped on board and saw a sign on the cabin door: *back in 5 mins, promise!* He decided not to attempt sitting in one of the flimsy-looking chairs, so took a Body Balm leaflet from a wicker table and stood reading.

We offer massage, pedicures, manicures, aromatherapy, detoxifying treatments, cupping and ear candling in our relaxing and soothing environment.
We are fully qualified masseurs so you are completely safe in our hands.

A half hour deep tissue massage was fifty pounds, he noted. There was a strong scent of lavender from a diffuser on the table, which set him sneezing and searching for a tissue.

A woman hurried on board, carrying a hessian bag full of brochures. She tripped as she stepped down and the brochures scattered over the floor. She was petite and blonde, her hair a confusion of fluffy waves. Spun sugar came to mind and he had a fleeting memory of the sickly taste of candyfloss.

'Oh, for goodness sake!' she said as she dropped the bag, more brochures tipping out. Swift bent to help her pick them up. Their heads collided briefly.

'Oh God, I'm so sorry. Are you Mr Swift?'

'That's right. I assume you are Isabella Alfaro. It's okay. Here you are.'

He put the brochures on the table, rescued the bag and handed it to her.

'Thanks so much. Sorry I kept you waiting but I had a call to say that these were ready. So . . .' she held out a hand in greeting.

She had a playful expression, an eager smile, neat pink lips and a button nose. She reminded him of a frisky kitten. He shook hands with her.

'Come inside,' she said. 'There are no clients for now so we can sit in.'

He followed her through a lace-curtained door into a warm, light room containing a massage table, a seated massage chair and a small hand basin with a shelf of oils, lotions and bottles of nail varnish above it. In one corner was a water feature, with a shallow greenish stone bowl set above a larger covered container. The lavender scent permeated the space and the tinkling music tinkled on. There were two white plastic chairs and she pulled one forward for him. She was wearing a rainbow-coloured crystal pendant at her neck. It refracted the light as she moved, glowing greens, oranges and yellows.

'Would you like a drink? Herbal tea or water?'

'No thanks, I'm fine. I want to ask you about Lisa and Dominic. I'm sorry about your friend, her death was shocking.'

'I was in pieces when I heard, I couldn't believe it. I was walking around as if I'd been bashed over the head. Her funeral was beautiful, very healing for everyone. She would have liked that. We placed a tiny piece of Azurite in her hands. It's known as "the stone of the heavens," you see. It soothes the soul. Native Americans used it to communicate with their spirit guides.'

Merrell with his wedding ring, Lisa with her heavenly nugget of copper. Isabella was playing with her pendant, twirling it between her fingers. She wore a long cream tunic over black leggings and she had kicked her pumps off outside the door. She drew her legs up on to the chair, her arms around her knees and gazed at him. Her finger and toenails were a distracting bright scarlet with sparkles.

'Do you think Dominic killed her?'

She put her chin on her knees. 'I know he didn't.'

'Pardon?'

She nodded. 'I just know.' She tapped over her heart. 'I know in here. Lisa used to say he was her bright spirit. Dom was an old soul, a good man. I did a back massage for him once and I could sense that he was full of positivity and love.'

Swift looked at her earnest expression. 'I've been told that he adored Lisa.'

'Oh yes. He was the nicest man she'd been with.'

'How long had you known her?'

'About five years. We met at a jewellery-making class. She was married to JoJo then. She was modelling but the work wasn't regular. We got chatting and had the idea for this business.'

'Did Lisa actually work here?'

'Oh no, she wasn't a therapist. She put up money to get us launched.'

'So did you know her husband?'

She ran a hand through her waves, fluffing them out. 'JoJo, yes, I knew him. He was okay but to be honest he was a bit flaky — gorgeous but she never knew what he was up to. She said he would do anything for money. He had big ambitions as a model but he never quite made the grade. There are loads of handsome men out there and you have to have something special to get beyond middle-of-the-road work.'

'Why did they split up?'

'Lisa had a thing with another guy. Richard Molina — she always called him Ricardo. He's in a band she sang with sometimes. JoJo threw a strop when he found out. He had quite a temper if he was crossed. They had a huge falling out. You know how it goes.' She focused on one of her toenails, rubbing the varnish. 'I don't know how this got smudged, it's so annoying.'

'Did Lisa cheat on Dominic?'

She looked at him as if she were trying to work out what answer he wanted. He was reminded of classmates who liked to please the teacher.

'Maybe. She never said, as such.'

'But it wouldn't surprise you?'

She tucked one leg under the other. The boat was moving gently on the water and she swayed with it. The lavender was blocking his nose.

'You see, Lisa was a free, generous spirit. I don't think she was made for monogamy. Some people aren't, they can't stand the confinement, can't breathe if they are locked down. And she was a terrible flirt. She said that about herself. She liked attention. Men were attracted to her and she liked being in love. She sort of couldn't stop herself.'

'And was she a free spirit with Perry who works here?'

'At one time, a couple of years ago, before Dom. He's married and he ended it.'

'Did she ever mention that she and Dominic argued?'

'Never, and I doubt they did. Dom was such an accepting kind of guy, the opposite of JoJo. He came here a few times to do some maintenance stuff. He was magic with electrics and plumbing and he was just so easy-going.'

'Were you at the party the night Lisa died?'

'Mm, it was full on, loads of people, booze flowing. She certainly knew how to throw a good one. She did love her parties, she must have had one every couple of weeks. I went along now and again.'

'Did you stay all night?'

'No, I got there around ten and left about one. It was still going strong then. Lisa was dancing for hours. She had amazing energy.'

The scented air, the warmth of the cabin, the gentle rocking of the boat, the trickling water and the hypnotic music were making him light-headed. It was hard to think straight. He pinched the bridge of his nose.

'Did you know other people there?'

'Not many. Richard and some of the band members were there and a couple of women from the salon where she had been a beautician — well, she just did facials really, nothing complicated. Perry turned up for a while. Lisa knew loads of people, you see, she kind of gathered them up as she went along, like the pied piper.'

'You didn't see her arguing with anyone?'

'No. Everyone was having a good time. Mind you, it was so jam-packed I don't suppose I'd have noticed if she was having a row.'

'What did Dominic make of the parties?'

She rolled her neck and straightened up. 'He never said. I mean, it was her flat and the parties were happening when he moved in. He was at some of them, but quite often he was at work. When he was there, he would creep away to bed at some point. I remember him saying he had ear plugs.'

She raised her head, pulling an imaginary string above it. 'This is the Alexander technique, good for aligning the spine. Have you ever tried it?'

'I have. It's helpful, as is any stretching. Did you know that Lisa had had an abortion?'

'God, no! Really? She must have been really fed up at having to do that. I'm sure she didn't want any more kids, she said pregnancy didn't do her figure any good.'

'How did she get on with Dominic's children?'

'She liked them, as far as I know. She said the oldest one was a bit moody sometimes. She didn't talk about them really, she left them to him. She wasn't a maternal type, I suppose.'

'Is that why her daughter went to live in Canterbury?'

'It was difficult, you know . . . things started to go wrong with JoJo soon after Tamsin was born. His mum seemed a good person to have the kid. I mean, a child is a massive responsibility and JoJo wasn't around much, travelling for work. Lisa said he went all old fashioned on her once she had given birth, seemed to expect her to stay at home, wear a pinny and be mumsy, bake biscuits. Shows how little he understood her. That was never going to happen.'

Swift felt fatigued by these misunderstandings and fractured lives.

'So, coming back to Dominic, you don't know of any dispute between him and Lisa, any reason why he might have been depressed?'

'No, don't think so. She said once that he had found something out or he had been told something that worried him.' She had reached for a bottle and cotton wool and started removing the nail varnish on the offending toe. A strong smell like paint stripper competed with the lavender.

'When was this?'

'Ahm, around last November I think.'

'Any idea what it was about?'

She leaped up, made a selection from the cosmetics on the shelf and deftly reapplied a coat of varnish. The abandoned cotton wool looked as if it had been used to staunch blood.

'Lisa didn't say. She said it was personal, like Dom was on a journey. He had found out this thing and he didn't want her to tell anyone. She did seem a bit excited about it. There, that will do. Don't want the customers thinking standards aren't high!'

Trying to keep this woman focused on a conversation was like herding cats. 'Do you think Dominic ever regretted getting together with Lisa and leaving his family? To be honest, they don't seem to have had much in common.'

'Not that I know of. I mean, he was all over Lisa, he really was. He bought her lovely stuff, took her on holiday. She showed me fantastic jewellery and clothes he'd got her. He was in deep, was Dom. Wish I could find a man to dote on me like that!'

More like out of his depth, buying things he couldn't afford. 'Okay, thanks. I'll leave you my card and if you think of anything else, do contact me.'

She rose quickly and quietly and moved behind him, rubbing her hands over his shoulders and the nape of his neck. Her fingers felt sure and strong. The sensation was not unpleasant.

'You should have a massage. You're very tense across here. I could sense tension in you the moment I saw you. Your energies are trapped. We have a slot right now.'

I'm probably tense because I can't breathe properly, he thought. 'Thanks, maybe some other time.'

'Do you want to offload any of your cares or worries or make a wish for the future?'

'Pardon?'

She stepped to the water feature. 'This is our well of wishes and worries.' She pointed to a slot in the lower container. 'You can write down your troubles or your hopes and put them in here. It's based on very old wisdom, you know. It's a form of healing.'

He recalled being taken to a holy well near his grandmother's house in Connemara when he was a child. He had closed his eyes and wished for a mountain bike while his mother murmured a prayer for his dying grandfather. Isabella was holding out a notepad. It was hokum, but then that played its part in life too. Why not, he thought. She went to the shelves and moved bottles around while he wrote, *health and happiness to Branna*, folded the paper and put it through the slot.

A man wearing jeans and a white T-shirt was on the deck, taking a phone call. He seemed agitated and he beckoned to Isabella, pointing a thumb down. A curvaceous girl with long legs and hair dyed a startling cherry red sat in one of the chairs, reading a magazine. She glanced up at Swift appraisingly, unwrapped a stick of chewing gum and put it in her mouth. Isabella offered him a couple of brochures as he left, saying he should give them to his friends.

Swift walked back towards King's Cross, breathing deeply, glad of the fresh air. He stopped to buy a coffee and sat on the grassy steps nearby, wondering what Merrell had discovered that was worrying him. Several people had now confirmed that something had been troubling the man, affecting his mood, and it seemed to be more than debt. The information could be significant but it was as insubstantial and hard to grasp as dust motes. His thoughts turned to Lisa and Isabella, two airheads running a business. He wondered how successful it was. There had been no customers during the time he was there and Isabella had seemed to lack the focus to run such an enterprise. He thought of Kris, a stab of pain engulfing him. She had set up her own business, making and selling beautiful fifties style clothes and other artefacts from the decade. She had been a pragmatic and imaginative self-starter, working as a waitress to fund her enterprise: no money from a rich father. If he had not met her, she would still be alive, sitting in her little top floor flat surrounded by rolls of material, poised over her sewing machine, listening to Polish radio. Sadness flooded him. He closed his eyes, regaining his composure.

He checked his email on his phone. He had received one from Nora Morrow: *Hi Ty, how you doing? Fancy a drink some time? I've been dumped, other than that, fine.*

Nora was a DI in the Met. He had met her while working on a previous case and had enjoyed her company. They'd had one date but things had not worked out because at the time he was helping Ruth through a miscarriage. Then Nora had got together with someone and the door had closed. It was months since Swift had seen her. Since Kris died, he had been staying in at night, listening to music, avoiding company. He had spent most of his time in Lyon on his own. Memories of her ambushed him; her nimble fingers, her laugh, the way she tapped the side of her nose when she was deep in thought. He knew Nora's understated style and thought she must be feeling raw and in need of a friendly ear. They could share a bottle of wine and sympathy. He replied: *Lovely to hear from you. Sorry about the dumping. I have those same scars. Let me know when you can meet.*

He finished his coffee and gave the Body Balm brochures to a couple of young men sitting nearby, telling them it was the place to go if their energies were trapped.

CHAPTER 6

It was hard to gauge how old Malory Meredith was. Early seventies, probably. She was slightly built, with shoulder-length hair the colour of parchment and wearing a woollen sheath dress of a multi-hued patchwork design with a roll-top neck. Her purple leather ankle boots had six-inch heels. Her eyes were a piercing blue, ringed with blue eye shadow and her lips shone with a shimmering pink gloss. Her hands trembled around her coffee, little involuntary spasms causing tiny spillages on the saucer. Her wrists and fingers were skin and bone. Swift found her remarkably beautiful in a frayed way.

Her flat was laid out in the same way as Lisa's, but filled with far too much furniture. Trinkets, vases and porcelain covered the shelves. Chairs and nests of tables were scattered about, many with piles of clothing, books or pictures perched on them. There were cabinets stuffed with china and jewellery. Badly hung, misaligned paintings covered the walls. Heavy brocade curtains made the living room resemble a dim cave where burglars had stashed their pickings, to be sorted out later.

Swift couldn't see anywhere to sit at first so stood by a tallboy heavy with dangerously stacked china, while Ms Meredith made coffee. It took her ages and when she reappeared, teetering on her heels, he took the dangerously rattling tray from her unsteady hands. She cleared magazines from an elegant walnut armchair for him and removed a couple of books from an intricately carved gold and black chair. It had a long back, a tapestry cushion embroidered with fleur de lis and what looked like a coat of arms on the top. She sat in it opposite him, as if enthroned.

'You've come about darling Lisa,' she said. Her voice was light and soft.

'Yes. Thank you for contacting me. Your neighbour upstairs said you knew Lisa well.'

Ms Meredith slowly picked her cup up, thought better of it and replaced it. 'She came and introduced herself to me the day she moved in, years ago. Brought me a bottle of very fine Sancerre, too. She was like a breath of fresh air. I knew at once that we would be good friends. I miss her terribly. She called in every day and we would chat. We had lunch every Wednesday. Just crackers and cheese on trays with a bottle of wine. We had so much in common, you see.'

There was a tiny crack in the bottom of Swift's cup. Coffee puddled into his saucer and he gave up trying to drink it.

'What kinds of things did you share?'

'Oh, so much really. For a start, we were both only children and daughters of doting fathers. We had both been models. She reminded me of my youth. She was vivacious and full of sparkle. There was never a dull moment when she was around.'

Swift suspected that Ms Meredith had quite a few dull moments nowadays. She had an air of solitude. She reached for a square yellow box with the logo Striped Tiger and selected a cheroot, which she proceeded to light.

The scented smoke it produced explained the trace of aniseed in the room.

'Lisa used to buy me these online,' she told him. 'I don't have a computer. I don't know what I'll do when I run out.' She looked at him as if she expected him to offer to procure them. When he didn't respond, she continued. 'We'd both had man trouble and of course she had a lovely singing voice, similar to mine.'

'You're a singer?'

She smiled a sad smile. 'Well, I used to be, until I had throat cancer and the pipes failed. I did a few musicals and backing work, some studio stuff too. I sang with Dusty Springfield once.' She hummed hoarsely, placing fingertips against her neck and he recognised *Son of a Preacher Man*.

'Great singer — Dusty. Did you ever hear Lisa sing with the band she worked with?'

'Not my kind of music but she threw herself into it. I used to listen to her practise scales. She had a pretty voice, soprano. She was self-taught but so enthusiastic. Always full of ideas, liked to try out new things. Oh, we would have a glass of wine and talk for hours! Time used to fly. She would suddenly say, "Now Malory, you're a terrible influence on me, I could stay here all day." Then she'd give me a kiss and speed away.'

She had sat back and was rubbing at the face of her jewel-encrusted watch, which looked expensive. Her eyes were quite rigid, he noticed. She rarely blinked.

'Tell me about the kind of man trouble Lisa had.'

She took a sip of coffee, manoeuvring the cup carefully to her lips. He held his breath. She placed it back down. Her left hand shook more than her right and she held it on her lap.

'You know, very beautiful men and women have a certain natural arrogance. I had it myself when I was young. I don't mean that they are necessarily disagreeable or narcissistic. It is just that because they are so attractive they are used to people admiring them. They know people are *looking* and they are accustomed to getting what they want. Lisa was like that. She knew the world would fall easily at her feet but she was disappointed when it refused to stay there. I know many people will speak ill of her to you, that she was a marriage breaker, a loose cannon, she caused unhappiness. And yes, she was and she did, but she was also susceptible emotionally. She had a hollowness inside that made her seek love and approval. She craved affection and that is a handicap in life. She wasn't just a predator, whatever people say. She was vulnerable too. Her beauty caused chaos. Yes, that would be true to say. Just as mine did in my time. Someone once said, "Beauty and folly are old companions." I agree.'

He waited to see if she was going to offer more information but she was focusing on her watch again, rubbing the glass face with her fingertip. Her cheroot lay burning in an ashtray in front of her so that he was seeing her through a bluish haze.

'You're a very attractive man,' she said then, gazing at him with those bright eyes. 'You have a certain enigmatic quality, a stillness. I'm sure you'll have been involved in some chaos.'

He appreciated her directness. 'I have. Maybe love always engenders chaos. But there's good, creative chaos and bad chaos.'

'And you don't always know which way the cards will fall. I like you, yes, I do. It is an instinctive thing, isn't it? You don't meet many people in life who you genuinely like. That's what I've found.' She relit her cheroot and sat back.

'Thank you. I understand that Lisa had quite a few men falling at her feet, including Dominic Merrell.'

'Oh, dear Dominic. Such a pleasant man but such a mistake.'

'How do you mean?'

'As soon as I met him I knew it wouldn't go well. He was easily led and she was so forceful. You could see that he was mesmerised by her. Also, he was really too *conventional* for Lisa. I didn't think he would hold her attention for long but she convinced herself that she needed someone like him, someone reliable and trustworthy. A number of men had let her down and JoJo, her husband, liked gambling. He would gamble on anything that moved and he persuaded her to part with huge amounts of money to fund his hobby. He was a man with trouble written all over him, but of course that is probably what attracted her. JoJo was a strong personality, more forceful than Lisa in some ways, pretty overbearing sometimes. I think that after him, Dominic's gentleness and malleability appealed. She was having some sort of problems with JoJo not long ago. She said he was doing her head in. He was here one day when Dominic was at work and she came down afterwards, very upset, saying they'd had a huge row.'

'They hadn't been together for a while though. Did she indicate what the row was about?'

'No, but she was agitated.'

'When was this?'

'Just after New Year, I think, sometime around then anyway.'

'How did other men let her down?'

'Well, Richard and Perry both said they would leave their wives, but they got cold feet. Perry moved in for a couple of weeks but then went back home.'

'But Dominic did leave his wife.'

'Yes. I suppose that meant he truly loved Lisa. Or didn't love his wife enough. Or was an utter fool. Possibly all three.'

'No one I have spoken to thinks that he killed Lisa. What's your view?'

'I think any of us could kill, given the right circumstances. There have been various experiments suggesting that. But I find it hard to believe of Dominic and I can't think of any reason why he would do it.'

'He found out she was unfaithful?'

'If she had been, and that was always a possibility with Lisa, I think he was the kind of man to desperately cling on to her rather than do away with her.' She looked at him. Her unblinking eyes were unnerving. She was a shrewd woman.

'I think I agree with you about that. I have been told that Dominic was depressed at times, and that there was something he had found out. Did Lisa say anything about that?'

'Around Christmas she told me that he had found out a secret to do with his family. I could see that she was bursting to tell me the whole story but she didn't, which was quite a feat for her. She was not one of nature's clams. It seemed to be something serious. She was lit up about it and I could see she was struggling to button her lip.'

'Lisa had a daughter, Tamsin.'

'Yes. Not a wanted child, you know, not really. Not a planned pregnancy, and I could see Lisa wasn't convinced about it. But JoJo was keen and then Lisa took up the idea. But once the baby was born, she quickly got bored with the routines and drudgery. That was Lisa, you see. Enthusiastic one minute, bored the next. She went back to work as soon as she could. She wanted a nanny but they didn't have enough money. There were big rows about that. Then JoJo came up with the idea of his mother looking after the baby. That child was in Canterbury before you could blink. I've never been a mother, but I'm not sure I could have parted with a tiny baby quite so easily.'

She closed her eyes and Swift drifted into his own thoughts about Ruth and Branna. Then he realised that Ms Meredith was looking at him, an eyebrow raised.

He sat forwards, focusing. 'Did you attend any of Lisa's parties?'

She shook her head. 'No. I don't go out, you see. I was mugged some time ago and I haven't wanted to leave this flat since. I must have been asleep the day you called. I can see that you have noted the tremor in my hands. It started after I was attacked. I prefer being inside now. I regretted not being able to attend Lisa's funeral. I sat here and raised a glass to her.'

'I'm so sorry. You must miss your friend from upstairs.'

'Yes. Well, there we are. I do miss the sound of her footsteps and that energy, that brio she always brought in with her. Would you like to meet Bertram? Lisa loved him. She'd pick him up and pretend to nibble his ear.'

'Bertram?'

'Come, come with me.' She took his hand in her cool grip and led him to a small room with a window overlooking the back garden. 'He's in here because this room is always quiet and shady and he mustn't have direct sun or heat.'

A large two-tier hutch was in the room, filled with hay, earthenware bowls and various tubes, pipes and cardboard boxes. A furry beige and cream creature with bright eyes was nibbling a piece of melon.

'Bertram, meet Mr Swift,' Ms Meredith said.

'Tyrone, please. Is he a guinea pig?'

'Well, then, call me Malory. Yes, that he is. Now we are all on first name terms. Lisa bought me Bertram after I was attacked, and all the equipment too. She had this picture of him done for my birthday. Dominic's wife was the artist and that is how Lisa met him. So the world turns.'

Swift looked at the framed picture on the wall. It was well executed, naturalistic. The portrait had shattered a marriage.

'Lovely,' he said. 'Lisa was very fond of you.'

'It was mutual. And I am so fond of Bertram, too. He should really have a companion but I couldn't deal with two animals. The tremor would get in the way too much.'

She opened the cage and picked him out gently, holding him close to her body with a hand beneath him. He looked around contentedly.

'He comes and sits on my lap in the evenings when I watch a film. He prefers westerns. Would you like to hold him?'

'I'd love to but I can be allergic to animal hair so I'll pass, if you don't mind.'

She rocked Bertram gently. 'I realise I'm a bit of a cliché — old woman talking to pet.'

'I don't think you believe that, Malory. I don't. We all find our consolations as we can. Mine is rowing on the river.'

She nodded, and put the guinea pig back in its hutch. It returned to its melon. Swift looked at a photo on the wall near Bertram's portrait. It was of Lisa and Dominic, the only one he had seen of them together. They were sitting on grass, arms around each other, both smiling. Dominic's hair was longer, he was unshaven and his glasses had retro tortoiseshell frames.

'It looks as if Dominic changed his image when he was with Lisa.'

'Oh yes, I suppose you would call it a more relaxed look. Well, he liked to keep up with her. She always wore the latest fashions. She never intended any harm, you know. She was intensely self-absorbed but also generous and kindly.' She turned to him, a spark in her eyes. 'Now, I've read lots of detective stories. This is where you ask me if there's anything else I can tell you.'

Swift laughed. 'Spot on.'

'There is something. I heard footsteps coming down the stairs on the morning Lisa died. I heard an engine, too, a bit like a motorbike but quieter, somewhere just up the street.'

'What time was this?'

'Some time after five a.m. I don't sleep well and I had just got back into bed after a glass of milk. My bedroom is at the front. I didn't think much of it at the time. I thought someone was leaving late after the party because the noise didn't die down until around four thirtyish. Then I heard the engine.'

'Did the police talk to you about this?'

'I mentioned it to a detective. But then Dominic said he was responsible so . . . it's probably of no importance. Although I can see that you think it might be.'

'Possibly. I am glad you told me. Did Lisa tell you she'd had an abortion some time recently?'

'No. Oh dear, do you think that might have had anything to do with what happened?'

'I don't know.'

'It's odd that she didn't tell me. She told me most things. Perhaps she thought I would find it upsetting. She knew that I'd had an abortion when I was young. It was botched and after that I couldn't have children.'

She led him to the front door, wobbling slightly on her high heels, her arm grazing the wall.

'This is as far as I go,' she said, opening several deadlocks. 'It has been a real pleasure to meet you. I hope you get to the truth of this awful matter.'

'It's been a pleasure to meet you too.'

'Could I ask a favour of you?'

'Of course.' He thought she was going to ask him to buy cheroots.

'Would you just give me a little hug? Lisa used to hug me every day, you see, and I find that is what I miss most. You are the only person I have met since she died that I would ask. Of course, I do miss conversation too. Sometimes I think I should get a lodger, I have a spare room, but how would I find someone?'

He stepped forward and leaned down, placing his arms lightly around her. She felt insubstantial. He was deeply moved. She breathed and gave a little sigh and a nod.

'Thank you.'

'Thank you, too. Can I ask you something else?'

'Go on.'

'Is Malory Meredith your real name?'

She giggled throatily. 'I was born Hester Cardew. I became Malory when I started modelling and I stayed Malory. Now you had better go before I tell you any more secrets.'

He turned as he walked up the road, knowing that she would be watching. She was and he waved. She had a dignity, a way of channelling her loneliness so that it did not define her. He hoped to see her again. Malory was the first person he had spoken to who threw light on Lisa as a rounded individual. She had been beautiful, self-centred and a woman who attracted and caused trouble, but also big-hearted and considerate. Steady, trustworthy Dominic Merrell, his wife's north star, had loved complicated Lisa and become a thief and a man with a family secret. She'd had an abortion and it may not have been his child. The more Swift learned, the less he understood. There were odd glimpses of a picture forming but it was blurred and shifting, like a half developed photo. JoJo Hayworth kept stepping forward, then back out of the frame. He had still featured somehow in Lisa's life, enough for them to row. And still there were those words that puzzled him, *a never-ending nightmare of blood and horror*. He needed to find a way through the confusion the couple had created between them and talk to the owner of an engine that sounded like a motorbike.

* * *

Swift had returned from a brisk row on the river. The sun was bright, the wind gusty. A cobweb-clearing day. He had pulled in at Chiswick for an apple. He decided to email Simone about a nagging thought that he had been turning over in his mind. She knew a fair amount about genetics and she liked to be asked to share her expertise. Anything that gained him brownie points with her could be deposited in the good-will bank and drawn on in future. She had replied by the time he got back to Tamesas. Given that it was Simone, it was a long-winded reply containing complex references to recessive and dominant alleles and proteins but confirmed what he had thought.

It occurred to him as he stowed his boat and made for home that he had not seen Cedric for a couple of days and should check on him. He had showered and was eating an avocado when he heard shouting from upstairs. His heart sank. Oliver was visiting. He ran upstairs, knocked on the door and pushed it open. Yana was sitting, or rather shrinking into Cedric's sofa with Oliver looming over her. She was wearing one of Cedric's diamond pattern jumpers, the sleeves rolled back. There was still a trace of bruising on her cheek. Cedric stood behind her, hands on hips, fierce-looking but white-faced.

'Is there a problem?' Swift asked.

Oliver turned and sneered. 'Oh, here's the cavalry. Why are you always sticking your unwanted nose in?'

Swift ignored him. 'Problem, Cedric?'

Cedric now had the shifty look Swift had noticed recently. 'Oliver objects to Yana being here,' he said.

'I object to her *living* here, moving in on you,' Oliver shouted. 'You know nothing about her. You could get into trouble with the police. People might think you're a dirty old man. How old is she, anyway?'

Swift took in the sleeping bag, blanket and pillow on the sofa. Yana coughed and looked terrified, her eyes huge and fixed on Oliver. Her hair was pulled back tight into a ponytail, emphasising the shadows of her face and the fading bruise near her eye. Swift had seen that look before in the faces of women he had worked with through Interpol, women who had been trafficked, abused, traumatised by daily brutality.

'Stop yelling and sit down,' Swift told Oliver. 'Yana is clearly frightened. It's okay,' he said to her quietly, 'no one is going to hurt you.'

Oliver stood where he was. Swift took a step towards him. 'I threw you out once before. Don't make me do it again. I probably would break your arm this time.'

Oliver threw himself into an armchair, knocking over Cedric's dominoes.

His father was rubbing his forehead with his thumb knuckle, leaving an imprint on the skin. 'I'm sorry, Ty. I should have let you know that Yana was here. I told her she could sleep on the sofa for a while. I had been thinking about her, worrying about her. I saw someone shouting abuse at her on the street a couple of nights back and I followed her to see where she was staying. She has been sleeping on a bench near the river and she has a nasty cough and a temperature. That's no life for a young girl. She needed proper food, warmth, a shower and clean clothing. Anyone with any decency would do the same.'

'Anyone with half a brain would realise what a stupid idea it was,' Oliver muttered. 'There are homeless shelters, soup kitchens and whatever, Dad. You're such a sitting duck for a sob story. She might have TB or hepatitis for all you know, or something worse.'

Yana got up. 'I go now. I'm sorry.'

'Don't,' Cedric said. 'Please, don't go back on to the street.'

'I make trouble,' she said.

'You certainly do,' Oliver agreed.

'Be quiet, Oliver!' Cedric told him. 'If you can't be civil, go away.'

Oliver looked taken aback at his father's stern tone. He lurched out of his chair. 'Have it your way but you're being incredibly stupid. Don't say I didn't warn you when she steals your stuff and it all goes tits up.'

At least she is not using threats and emotional blackmail to extract money from an old man, Swift thought. They listened to Oliver clatter down the stairs. The house reverberated as he banged the front door. Cedric gestured to Yana to sit and sank down beside her.

Swift pulled up the chair Oliver had vacated. 'What's the story?' he asked.

'Yana, do you want to tell Tyrone or shall I?'

The girl shrugged. 'You tell,' she said listlessly, coughing again.

Cedric ran his hands over his eyes. 'Yana and her brother escaped from Aleppo after the rest of their family were killed. They spent over a year in refugee camps. Her brother had leukaemia so they came here under the vulnerable person resettlement scheme. They were given a room in a house in Bolton and her brother started treatment. It had been left too late and he died within months of arriving here. Some men hanging around the house offered her work so she went to the address they gave her. It turned out to be a brothel and she was locked in and made to work there. She managed to escape and came to London a couple of months ago. She was studying music in Aleppo. Her English is slow but improving all the time.'

Yana held her chest, coughing. 'I learn many insults,' she said, looking up.

There was some strength left in her gaze. Swift thought she might stand a chance.

'I can imagine,' he told her. 'You should see a doctor.'

'I've made an appointment for later today with my GP. She said she'll see Yana as a temporary patient,' Cedric said.

'I can't play well with cough,' Yana said, gesturing to her flute.

'I think you should stay here until we can help you sort something out,' Swift told her. 'You are here legally, which helps. As well as dealing with your cough, you should ask the woman doctor to check you over, check your general health. You've been through a lot. Do you understand what I mean?'

She nodded. 'I understand.' She turned to Cedric. 'Will your son come back and shout at me again?'

'No,' Cedric said. 'He can only visit if he promises not to shout. I am sure he will understand when he thinks it over. He's not a bad lad at heart.'

Hope springing eternal in the fond father, Swift thought, remembering Donald Eastwood's unstinting praise of his daughter. Would he be like this with his own daughter in years to come, making excuses for her no matter what she did or how she behaved?

'Yana, we should report this place in Bolton to the police,' he said.

She shook her head violently. 'No! No police!'

'You're frightened that those men will come after you.'

'Yes. They tell us, you talk, you are punished.'

'I understand but the police can protect you. What about the other girls who are still there?'

She shook her head, drawing her arms into her body, making herself as small as possible.

'Okay, okay. We'll leave it for now. But please think about it. And please don't tell anyone where you're staying. Understand? That's important.'

She nodded and was silent, head down. She had clearly learned it was the best way to try to evade notice.

CHAPTER 7

Swift wanted to meet JoJo Hayworth as soon as possible. He seemed to have been more than a match for Lisa and there was evidence of a recent falling out as well as a significant inheritance. He didn't answer his phone or reply to messages. When Swift called his mother, she said he was away working in Denmark and wouldn't be back until the following week.

In the meantime, Swift had arranged to see Richard Molina. His office was on the sixth floor of a narrow, Dickensian-looking building in a back street near Edgware Road. The yellowish bricks were dull from traffic pollution and several of the ground-floor sash windows had cracked glass. He had told Swift that he was a lecturer in Business Studies and had a free period after lunch. The college he worked at was a private institution called the Cornel Academy. It offered various degree courses including MBAs and qualifications in accounting and finance and had links with universities in Asia. A stained, laminated notice inside the door stated, *One Capital City. World Influence.*

The shabby foyer was busy with students, mainly young men, their voices bouncing off the high ceilings in a maelstrom of languages and accents. The building itself was a honeycomb of corridors with lino-covered floors, peeling paint and that smell of boiled cabbage that often prevails in such airless places. Swift took the crowded lift and looked for room 6C, finding it midway along a narrow, gloomy corridor. A voice shouted for him to come in when he knocked and he entered a tiny room almost filled by a desk heaped with files and books.

Molina was crouched over a computer but stood to shake hands, taking off his blue tinted glasses and propping them on top of his head. 'Welcome to academia. Not quite the dreaming spires of Oxford, but we do our best.'

'I'm sure you do. Business certainly seems to be thriving, judging by the heaving humanity everywhere.'

'Yep. Everyone wants an MBA these days. Management has taken over the world.'

He was a slim, slightly built man with mahogany skin, long black hair tied back in a ponytail, a thin moustache and a broad forehead. His spindly fingers were nicotine stained. He wore jeans and a denim shirt. His smile was engaging and whimsical, as if he looked on the world and found it amusing.

'Pull out that chair,' he said. 'I'll just save this document.'

The room looked out on to the brick wall of the building next door. The open window admitted the hum of traffic. There was a damp patch below the window ledge and the magnolia paint had seen better days. Swift thought Molina must be in his late forties and wondered what career path had brought him to this cramped room in a third rate college. He watched him peer through his smoky glasses at the screen. He seemed an unlikely member of Brainscan, but middle-aged men often tried to relive their youth.

Molina closed his computer screen and shifted a file to one side. 'You've come about Lisa?'

'That's right. I understand you had a relationship with her and she sang in your band.'

'Correct on both counts. The relationship was quite a while ago. She sang with us now and again, when the fancy took her. An ad hoc arrangement.'

'If Dominic Merrell didn't kill her, have you any idea who might have?'

'Wow! He confessed, didn't he?'

'He did. But he may not have done it.'

Molina put his hands behind his head. He had discerning eyes. 'I only met him once. He seemed docile. I don't know why anyone else would have done it. She was a sweet kid. Crazy and needy but sweet.'

'She had quite a few relationships. She wanted you to leave your wife?'

'We talked about it. I couldn't in the end. Ties that bind. I wasn't prepared to unpick everything, put my kids through that. Also, I was too old for her and she was immature.'

'Maybe she got involved with someone who found her crazy and too demanding rather than sweet. People who break up relationships aren't always popular and she made her way through a few.'

'True. She liked to try to mould people to what she wanted. So she called me Ricardo and Dominic became Nico. No one else called him that and the name didn't suit him. But that was how she wanted it, so . . .'

'Was she involved with Harry Merrell?'

Molina sat forward and looked intently at Swift. 'I don't know. She had blurred boundaries so . . . possible. I didn't pick up on that kind of vibe, though. I got the impression she had decided to make a project of Harry. She was whimsical in that way. She would take someone up like a hobby, the way other people take up pottery or rug making. She seemed fond of him in a big sister fashion and of course he was a bit in awe of her. He probably fancied her and felt confused. Lisa was like a kid in a sweet shop with men and she liked to pick-and-mix. She was impulsive. Once she got an idea in her head, it had to happen. You could say she had no middle gear.'

'She told Harry he might get some work with Brainscan?'

'Yeah. She brought Harry along to a rehearsal once, asked me to try him on drums but I said no. I have a good drummer. I thought it was just another one of her whims and it would cause trouble. Also, the kid was awkward and sulky looking. I didn't think he would fit in. We have a good vibe in the band and I wasn't going to upset it for her. She wasn't pleased, grumbled about it for a couple of weeks. Like I said, she liked to take people along for the ride.'

Swift weighed this up. 'Do you think his father knew Harry was with her on that occasion?'

'No idea. If he did, he might not have minded. After all, she was a sort of stepmother to Harry so Dominic might have liked that she was taking an interest. I met Dom at one of her parties. Quiet, introspective kind of guy. Head over heels in love with her. I thought he was good for her, might stabilise her, but she was already getting tired of him.'

Swift was warming to Molina. He seemed self-possessed and smart. Straightforward, too. 'Did she tell you that?'

Molina nodded. He cleared paperwork from one side of the desk, dumping it on the floor, and put his feet up on it. He was wearing white leather winkle-picker boots.

'After we stopped sleeping together, Lisa decided I'd be a father figure. Or maybe that was the attraction all along, that I was twenty years older. She would seek me out for a heart to heart now and again. Sometimes she would call in here, sit in that chair you are in and tell me her troubles. She was worried about the business she was involved in, that boat on the canal. Said it was losing money and there were other problems.'

'She didn't specify?'

'No, that was Lisa for you. She would feed you snippets of things. But she said she was thinking of shutting the business down and the woman she owned it with disagreed, and they'd had a falling out. Lisa didn't like arguments, she was used to getting her own way. She was a bit peevish the night of that last party, fed up with how her life was shaping. She told me JoJo was annoying her. She wanted him to repay her some of the money she had given him over the years because she needed it to patch up her business, but he wouldn't play ball. She was naïve in that way. Why would the guy cough up when he didn't have to? And she was fed up with Dominic. She took me into a corner of the kitchen and moaned about him, saying he was no fun anymore, that he was morose a lot of the time and fretting about money. He was also caught up with some complicated family stuff that was getting him down and doing her head in. I presumed she meant he was having guilt pangs about the wife and kids he dumped for her.'

'Did you offer sympathy?'

'No. She got huffy with me because I told her she should stop playing games and she needed to stick it out this time, face reality. The guy had left his marriage and his home for her, the least she could do was see him through the bad times. She both liked and disliked me because I didn't indulge her. As far as I could make out, her own father always gave her everything she wanted, so I was a novelty, the bad cop to Daddy Eastwood's good cop.'

'A man called Perry also left his wife for her.'

'Perry Wellings, yeah, but only briefly. He works part-time in the therapy business, doing massage. He was at that last party and I had the idea that she was sniffing around him again. I'm not sure he would have gone for her a second time, though. He has a fiery daughter who gave him hell about his playing away the first time, threatened never to speak to him again etc.'

'How about the other members of Brainscan? Did Lisa have any personal involvements with them?'

'Unlikely. Brad and Gary are gay and Rhoda is straight and married.'

'Did you see Lisa argue with anyone at the party?'

'No. She was drunk and high but the vibe was all okay. I left about three and it was still going strong.'

'Was Perry Wellings still there?'

'I couldn't say. I was pretty wasted by then.'

'Lisa had an abortion shortly before her death. It wasn't your baby?'

'Absolutely no way.'

'Any ideas?'

He held his hands out. 'Dominic's, I guess. But with Lisa and her complicated life . . . I can tell you, she wouldn't have wanted more kids. She didn't have much time for Tamsin, the one she had. Her idea of mothering was to visit Tamsin now and again with presents. Hit and run. You know, man, you've got your work cut out if you really think Dominic didn't kill her.'

Sometimes cases resolved through dogged questioning and following threads, sometimes because of a lucky break. Swift had no sense which way this one might unravel.

'It's beginning to feel that way. Thanks for your help. Have you been in Brainscan for long?'

'I started it five years ago. Keeps me sparking and involved and it's as different as can be from the world of management science and organisational behaviour. I write all the songs, spend my evenings messing about with my guitar.'

Swift nodded. 'One last question. Do you ride a motorbike or scooter?'

'I wish. I used to have a Harley but I sold it years ago. My easy rider days are behind me. I'm in a hatchback now, domesticated and neutered, driving to the supermarket for the weekly shop.'

'Do you know any of Lisa's friends who owns one?'

'Harry Merrell has a scooter. She rode on the back of it that time she wanted me to try him out on the drums. I tell you, he was pretty pissed off when I turned him down. I think Lisa had spun him a line that it was pretty much a done deal, so I had some sympathy. He reminded me of some of my students when I fail their work. One of those young men who looks like an adult but hasn't quite left adolescent moping behind.'

He smiled, laughing to himself, and tapped his keyboard to wake up his computer.

* * *

Harry Merrell was loping down the road in front of Swift, hands deep in the pockets of his bomber jacket, rucksack bumping against his broad back. He was talking to a girl in tight grey jeans and a short cream wool coat with a fur collar. Strands of thick cherry red hair fell about her shoulders. They parted company and she headed up a side road. Swift quickened his pace and caught up with Harry before he reached home.

'Hi there, can I have a word?'

Harry turned. 'What are you doing here?'

'I just wanted a chat with you. I've been talking to quite a few people about your dad.'

'So?' He looked at the ground.

'So I was curious,' Swift said mildly. It was worthwhile taking a stab in the dark, and Harry's truculence was beginning to grate on him. 'Why were you at Lisa's the night she died?'

He hefted his rucksack. There was a distinct flinch. 'You what?'

'You were there with your scooter. Were you at the party?'

'No, I fucking well wasn't. I wasn't anywhere near that fucking bitch.'

'Oh, she was a bitch? I didn't know you felt that strongly about her, Harry. Although Adam did say you called her a fake.'

A silence fell. There was an ambulance wail from nearby and a window cleaner across the street rattled a ladder. Swift kept a steady gaze on Harry's flushed face.

'I know you gave Lisa a lift on your scooter at least once, when you were turned down for a try-out with Brainscan. Why was she a bitch, Harry? Did she come on to you? You're a good-looking young man and she liked to flirt. Or maybe it was just that she fed you a line, made promises about an opportunity with the band that she couldn't keep. That would be pretty annoying and disappointing. I wonder, did your dad know about your little outing together? Maybe there was more than one outing.'

'You can take your half-baked ideas and shove them where the sun don't shine. I wasn't anywhere near her.'

'Where were you the night of the party?'

'At a friend's.' His eyes were cloudy with pain.

'Can I have their name?'

Harry's fist was clenching in his pocket, his jaw muscles working overtime. 'No. Now fuck off.'

He walked to the house and opened the garage door. Swift followed, watching as he threw his rucksack in a corner, flicked on an electric wall heater and sat at his drum kit. He stretched the fingers on each hand, palms facing away, pulling them gently towards his body, then took a drumstick with both hands and rolled it up and down.

Swift propped himself against the Vespa. 'I'm not sure about your rudeness and your foul language, Harry. It seems like a front. I think there is a pleasant young man hiding in there. I would say he's frightened, worried. I know you are grieving. My mother died when I was a bit younger than you and it's hard going. But I reckon you know more than you're saying. I think it is possible that your dad didn't murder Lisa. Surely you want to help your mother and help me if that might be true?'

Harry turned away, arched his huge feet against the wall and leaned into them.

'Maybe you're protecting your mother,' Swift added. He ran his hands over the scooter's handlebars. 'Maybe you don't want her to be hurt anymore, and truth hurts. That girl you were just with, is she something to do with Body Balm?'

The young man took a drumstick and brought it down with a crash on a cymbal. 'You're wasting your time, Mister Detective. I've got nothing to tell you.'

'Not even that Lisa had had an abortion?'

Harry stared at him, a confused but challenging look, then took both drumsticks and launched into a deafening roll.

Swift considered the handsome cleft chin, then exited the garage and rang the doorbell. Georgie Merrell answered after a second ring, looking tired and distracted. She was wearing jeans, woolly socks featuring Spiderman, and an old check shirt with streaks of oily crayon on the sleeves.

'Oh, sorry, I wasn't expecting you. I'm just in the middle of some work and I've got a deadline . . .'

'It's okay, I apologise for disturbing you. I just wanted to ask you two questions, if that's okay. I don't need to come in.' The puppy had appeared behind her, barging against her legs.

'Oh, you'd better or Sid might get out and then all hell would break loose. Come up to my studio, and then we'll escape the worst of the drumming too.'

Her studio was in the smallest bedroom, at the back of the house and on the opposite side to the garage. A faint thudding could still be heard below the Bach she was playing. Sid had followed them up and sat obediently in a bed under a bookcase. Animal portraits of all sizes and in a variety of frames filled the walls. Cats seemed to predominate but there were dogs, horses, ponies, rabbits, sheep, goats, hamsters and birds.

'Do you work in different mediums?' Swift asked.

'I can pretty much turn my hand to whatever's wanted so I provide water colour, oils, pastels, pencil drawings.'

'I saw the portrait you did of a guinea pig for Lisa. She gave it to her downstairs neighbour.'

Georgie pulled a wry face. 'Ah yes, the start of my downfall.' She picked up a stained cloth and rubbed her fingers on it. Her easel held a work in progress, three sleeping Alsatians in oils.

He started with what he thought would be the least stressful question. 'Was your husband adopted?'

She held the cloth and stared at him. 'What an odd question! Unexpected, too. He never mentioned that he had been, no. What makes you ask?'

'I saw the photo downstairs of your wedding. Dominic had a cleft chin, which Harry has inherited. Neither of his parents had a cleft chin.'

'What does that mean? You've lost me.' She sat on her adjustable stool, the fine skin on her forehead wrinkling.

'I consulted a friend who confirmed that although two parents without cleft chins can have a child with a cleft chin, it's rare. So I thought maybe Dominic had been adopted. I've been hearing that he had discovered some family secret which might lend itself to the theory.'

'Well . . . I just don't know. He never said anything about any of this. You would think he would have mentioned something in all the years we had been together . . . I mean, it is an important thing in life. His parents never hinted at it either. Unless he didn't know. Maybe his adoptive parents never told him and he found out somehow.'

'Maybe.'

'But even if he was adopted, how is that relevant to what has happened?'

'It might not be. It's just part of the picture, possibly.'

'Surely it can't be true? It's the kind of thing you'd talk about.'

'I don't know. Perhaps some people wouldn't think it important.'

Sid gave a soft bark, more like a grumble, his ears up.

'He knows it's nearly time for Adam to come home,' Georgie said.

Swift moved and looked out of the window on to the back garden. Part of the neighbour's fence was broken and was leaning in. The next-door garden was unruly, filled with ground elder, weeds, a stack of plastic chairs and a rusting lawnmower. He turned round. Georgie was polishing a silver frame. The smell of the liquid she was using reminded him of his mother. She used to clean a pair of antique candlesticks every Christmas, in preparation for their annual outing onto the dinner table. His mother had rarely worn make-up but she used to put on a dark red lipstick in the winter months to cheer up the gloomy days. He could see her, the dash of colour on her lips, blowing her hair back from her forehead as she polished. He felt ambushed by the flash of memory and moved by it. He touched the edge of Georgie's desk to bring himself back to the present.

'I've found out that Lisa had an abortion shortly before she died,' he told her.

She looked at him, fresh sorrow in her eyes, then returned to her rubbing at the frame. She took her time replying. 'Well, it can't have been Dominic's child. He had a vasectomy after Adam was born.' She shook her head. 'I wonder if he knew. That would have been shocking for him, an awful betrayal.'

'It would. If he found out, he might have been very angry. Proof of disloyalty only a couple of years into the relationship. Maybe he knew and that's why he seemed depressed.'

'I just don't know, Mr Swift. I was no longer his confidant. Poor Dominic.'

'One last thing. The night Lisa died, was Harry at home?'

She shook her head. 'He was staying at a friend's that night. He came back around mid-morning the following day, I think.'

'Do you know which friend?'

'No. Harry is old enough to come and go as he pleases. Why do you ask?' She stood fidgeting with her shirt cuffs, looking worried.

'I just wondered. I've asked lots of questions but he doesn't want to communicate with me.'

'I'm sorry. He has been like a different person in the last couple of years. We used to laugh and joke . . . now he behaves as if I'm invisible and I barely get a nod from him. I don't have the energy to challenge him about it. I have no idea what he is thinking or doing. Dominic struggled too, I know. I hold on to the fact that his studies are on track. I'll be relieved when he goes away to college later this year. I think it will be good for all of us. Does that sound terrible?'

He looked at her drained expression. 'I suspect lots of parents feel the way you do. Going away will do him good. He needs to assert himself, grow into himself fully. And you'll get a break from the drums.'

She smiled a weary smile. 'It's just that when you're on your own with no one to discuss your worries with . . . they multiply, cluster around you. No one to tell you you're being daft, getting things out of proportion.'

He didn't know if her worries about her eldest son were daft or warranted. He hoped the former.

'Adopted . . . surely, that can't be the case.' She pressed her lips together. 'Dominic seemed so close to his parents, they had a real bond. I can't believe that he wouldn't have shared something like that with me.'

'I don't know if he was,' Swift told her. 'It's worth looking into, that's all.'

He left her tidying her studio. As he went downstairs, he paused and looked again at the wedding photo, wondering if it held explosive secrets.

On the way back to the station, he rang Finbar Power to ask if Dominic or his parents had ever mentioned adoption. It took a long time for the call to be answered and he was about to give up when Power picked up. He sounded jaded and puzzled, asking him to repeat the question. Then he answered slowly, his voice strained. No, he said, he had never heard any suggestion of adoption, no hint at all. As far as he knew, Dominic had been brought up by his birth parents and had been close to them. "They were a tight, united unit," he added.

CHAPTER 8

The Parterre in Notting Hill was Nora Morrow's favourite bar. She had told Swift she liked its Eastern bazaar décor, battered leather armchairs with escaping shreds of stuffing and the low lighting. The scuffed floorboards creaked authentically and the patchy, velvet-covered benches had plump gold cushions with tassels. Swift had not been sleeping well, thinking of Ruth and the baby and how they were going to work things out, if at all. Emlyn Williams was making the right noises but the reality of living with a child who was not his might alter his tune. Swift had lain awake in the early hours, his mind racing, not least of which was would he be any good as a father? He knew nothing about babies, except that they were fragile, demanding and a huge responsibility.

Swift had a blister on his right hand from his recent row and he rubbed it gently as he waited for Nora. He was tempted to stretch out on one of the benches with a cushion under his head. Jazz was playing softly, the upbeat kind that you heard on the soundtracks of sixties films. He sipped his merlot and read an email from Donald Eastwood:

Hi Mr Swift, I'm back in Cape Town. I've got quite a headache here. I've found out that Body Balm is in a load of trouble. I've been copied into a solicitor's letter. Someone got badly injured during one of the treatments and they've got themselves a lawyer. They're going to sue. I wish Lisa had told me about this. Seems she kept a lot from me. To be honest, I've taken a look at the books and the business hasn't been doing anything like as well as I thought. I reckon any damages in a court case would wipe it out. I've been trying to get hold of Isabella Alfaro but she hasn't come back to me about it. Anyways, I don't know if this is relevant but I thought I'd let you know.

Troubles certainly followed Lisa and Merrell. He was spoiled for which one to focus on, theories crowding his brain. Lisa was fascinating and elusive. She'd had her fingers in many pies and had blazed a trail through plenty of lives and marriages. There were a number of players in this drama. He needed to order his thoughts and made a list while waiting for Nora:

Dominic Merrell: Debts and something troubling about his family. Depressed. Out of his depth with Lisa. May have known Harry was hanging out with her. If he knew about abortion, angry. Maybe adopted but how is that relevant?

Lisa: Caused conflict and desire. Business in trouble. Rowed with Isabella and Hayworth. Tired of Merrell. Pregnant by someone. Involved with Harry or Perry Wellings or yet another man. Wanting money back from Hayworth.

Any of these could be a reason for wanting her gone.

The party. Isabella, Molina and Wellings were there and could have used the opportunity.

Nora appeared, dressed in her usual work apparel, a smart grey suit and one of her collection of quirky string bow ties. Tonight it was indigo with a pattern of tiny crescent moons in a lighter blue. She kissed him on the cheek, slung down a laptop and rucksack, unlaced her smart black trainers and kicked them off as a waiter approached.

'Shall we have a bottle?' she asked Swift.

'Is it that kind of evening?'

'Certainly is.' She told the water to bring a bottle of whatever Swift was drinking and some nibbles. She loosened her tie and smiled at him, her grey-green eyes clear and glowing. 'Been looking forward to this,' she said. 'Give me a glug from your glass while we're waiting.'

He held it out to her. 'It's good to see you.'

'Yeah. You too. Been on the river?'

'Of course. All seasons, all weathers.'

The bottle arrived with tiny bowls of nuts and pretzels, and they clinked glasses.

'Sláinte,' Nora said, taking a large mouthful and closing her eyes. 'It's been a shit day. This is bliss.'

They shared an Irish heritage. Nora was from Dublin and Swift's mother came from Connemara. She had seemed familiar to him from their first meeting, with her strong face and quick wit. They sat in a companionable silence for a few minutes, and then Nora unshelled some pistachio nuts and held them out in her palm.

'I heard that you're going to be a daddy. Is that right?'

'Who told you that?' He ate a couple of nuts. Their saltiness went well with the wine.

'Mark Gill. I met him at a conference.'

Mark was an old friend of Swift's who had worked with him in the Met. 'Well, he's right. I'm expecting a girl in June.'

'And the mammy is the woman you were once engaged to, right?'

'Ruth, yes. It's complicated.'

'Everything's bloody complicated. I heard a bit about what happened to you. Is it true that that poor Polish woman you were seeing was murdered just as your cousin got married?'

'Yes. Her name was Kris. She failed to turn up to the wedding. I went to her flat and found her. She had been strangled . . . I, I miss her.'

'And now, let's see. Yer man who Ruth is married to was behind the murder?'

'How do you know all this? From Mark?'

'Mainly. But I know Alexa Markham, too. She was on Kris's murder investigation, right? She has just been promoted. Good woman, that one.'

'Right. Well, that about sums it up. You seem to know all about me.'

'I'm a good detective, I do my homework,' she said softly. 'Well, Ty, you've been through the mill and no mistake. Where's Ruth now?'

'Back with her husband in Brighton. The baby's fine, that's the main thing.'

'We have to find ways to comfort ourselves, don't we? Find little positives amongst life's debris.' She poured them both another glass and popped a handful of peppery pretzels in her mouth, dusting her hands off.

'And how do you find your comfort, Nora? Not just from a bottle and nibbles?'

'Oh, you know, at the gym, reading sad books, chocolate, of course and sitting on buses. All sources of consolation.'

'Buses?'

'Mm. I just get on any bus and see where it goes. It's very relaxing, I can recommend it. I have seen all kinds of fascinating sights from the top deck. I got a 36 from Park Lane last Sunday. Double decker therapy, I call it.' She hitched another chair up and put her feet on it. She had a knack of making herself at home.

'You said you were dumped. What happened, was it that blond guy I saw you in here with?'

'Yep, Alistair. It was all going so well. Then he told me he had been offered a job in New York and he had accepted it. He didn't think a long distance relationship would work etc. etc. I think he liked me but not my career. So, there we are. He's in the Big Apple now and I still get to take the 36 bus to New Cross.'

'His loss, Nora. Cheers to you and hope he gets whatever he deserves.'

She nodded. 'As my grandmother would have said, "May he find the bees but miss the honey." She had a good store of curses, one for every occasion. Are you hungry? I'm starved and they do good fish and chips.'

They ordered food and another bottle of wine. Her grandmother's curse reminded him of the well at Body Balm and he told her about it and his reason for going there as they ate and drank. He had not drunk so much since Kris died and he was enjoying it and Nora's company too much to slow down.

'I recall that Merrell case,' Nora said, her voice heavy with the wine. 'That's a meaty one to get your teeth into. Any suspects so far, apart from Merrell himself?'

'I'm wondering about his son who is twitchy and might have taken against his glamorous stepmother. Merrell and Lisa, the stabbed woman, were both in financial trouble and I think Merrell had discovered something about being adopted but I don't know what yet. Lisa might have been having an affair. She'd had an abortion. Then there is a JoJo Hayworth, Lisa's husband, who seems to have been money grabbing and troublesome. I'm working on it. It feels as if I'm trying to grasp running water at times.'

'It might be the unlikely and unusual, just for once: perhaps a random stranger stabbed her, someone who wandered in during the party.'

'I don't think so. I have the feeling this is close to home but in a number of ways. This is multi-layered.'

They talked on until late. The fish and chips were terrific, hot and crispy, accompanied by pungent garlic mayonnaise.

'Why does food taste better when you're drunk?' Nora asked.

'Maybe because judgement is blunted. But this is great, drunk or not.'

Three bottles of wine down, Nora yawned and smiled blearily at him, pushing her hair out of her eyes. His head was singing and she was out of focus.

'You were going to ask me out last time we were in here, weren't you?'

'Yeah. Then Alistair arrived.'

'And the time we went rowing, that was a kind of date but then someone phoned you. Was that Ruth?'

'Yes. She'd just had a miscarriage.'

'And now I'm footloose again but you've got Kris on your mind and an immin . . . imminent birth and a sort of long distance ménage à trois, so I guess you're preoccupied.'

'Yeah.'

'Am I slurring as much as you?'

'Yeah.'

They laughed and he took her hand. 'We keep mis . . . mistiming.'

'Yeah. Oh God, I'm pissed as a newt. Better get a taxi.'

She told him he had been a tonic and kissed him on the lips, a warm, soft, winy kiss as she climbed into her cab. He hailed one shortly after and slumped back into the seat. Outside his house, the driver had to shake him from a deep slumber.

'This isn't air b an' b on wheels, mate. Wakey-wakey!'

He woke at four a.m. with a raging thirst. He couldn't remember getting into bed but he could recall Nora's warm lips on his.

* * *

Swift arrived in Canterbury in Cedric's car, a burnt orange Mini Cooper convertible. Cedric drove it so rarely that it still smelled of new leather. The day was mild, with storm clouds overhead and a warm, squally wind. Mrs Hayworth lived in a shabby street of terraced houses with narrow pavements and dustbins standing by each front door. It lacked trees, greenery or any other redeeming feature. What must stylish Lisa have made of this? The house was rendered and painted white, with a front door of chalky blue. There was a low brick wall fronting it. At least a dozen ceramic butterflies of different sizes were attached to the house front, a blaze of yellows, pinks and blues, some with spots like polka dots. It was a striking sight and certainly threw the neighbours into drab relief. Swift rang the bell. He was looking forward to meeting the owner.

She was heavily made up, with thinning, purplish hair coiled in a French pleat, a white and orange floral print cardigan, faded blue jeans with cloth roses sewn on and white plimsolls. She told him to call her Cora, addressed him as my love and led him through a butterfly-themed hallway into a back room that had been knocked through into the kitchen. There was a smell of bacon mixed with air freshener. There were more butterflies on the walls and covering most of the surfaces. They were made of ceramic, glass, pottery, fabric and paper.

'I adore my butterflies,' she said unnecessarily.

'They're certainly striking.'

'You sit down, my love. Come from London, have you? Want a cuppa?'

'I'm okay for now, thanks. Is your son here?'

'He'll be back soon. He took Tammy to the play park. I'm surprised she remembered who he is.'

This was said with a certain satisfaction. She had a hard face, although she did not seem unkind and he suspected she had been worn down by life. Her skin was deeply lined beneath the tan make-up and it had settled into the furrows on her forehead. Her mouth was a thin line. She looked like a woman who had given up hoping for much.

'Your son doesn't see much of Tamsin, then?'

'No, nowadays he's hardly ever here. Always off to different places with his work, he says. Poor little mite Tammy is. Never saw much of her mother either. At least it means she doesn't miss her now she's gone. I suppose it's just as well she's got me, my love.'

'It can't be easy for you, looking after a little one. You're on your own?'

'Oh yes, my hubby died ages ago. Too right, it isn't easy. I thought I'd done my child rearing, had a bit of time to myself at last. Then Tammy came along and I was lumbered.' She glanced around, as if someone might be listening. 'Lisa didn't want her, you know. She was all for an abortion.'

'That must have been difficult.'

'Hmm. JoJo persuaded her not to, said he'd like a kid. I reckon he thought it would settle her down, make her into the wife he wanted. I could have told him he had that wrong. But he doesn't listen to me, thinks I'm old and daft. Maybe I am daft but I know a thing or two, and Lisa was a good-time girl. Nappies and night feeds cramped her style. I mean to say, a baby changes your life, doesn't it? Then as soon as Tammy was a couple of months old, Lisa wanted to go back to work and got herself a job without telling JoJo. He came here and persuaded me to look after Tammy. Said they would make sure I was okay for money, although sometimes I've had to remind him. She's a nice kid but it's tiring at my age. I'm sixty-eight, you know.

Then of course they split up and her mother only came here every couple of months. She didn't like me calling the kid Tammy, said she would rather I didn't shorten her name. Cheek of her! But that was Lisa all over. I thought, you want her called Tamsin, you take her home and look after her yourself. I kept my mouth shut for JoJo's sake. That Mr Eastwood is ever so nice. He sends me money regular. He's a gentleman. Means I can get a babysitter and go to my club or to bowls. I love my bowls.'

He could understand that she would feel imposed on, having to employ a babysitter in her late sixties. He wondered what kind of life the child had, on her own with this reluctant grandmother. There were no toys lying around. The place was a curious mixture of traditional dark pine cupboards and shelving and worn woodchip wallpaper with a large wall-mounted plasma TV, new-looking armchairs and bright kitchen gadgets. He guessed that she used her unexpected income to indulge herself, and that Tamsin was a mixed blessing.

'Did you get on with your daughter-in-law?'

She laughed. It was a rough sound, snappy. 'I never saw that much of her, my love. She was a flighty piece, I know that. She was all charm when she wanted something. I reckon she knew I had the measure of her so she gave me a wide berth. She never stayed more than an hour when she came to see Tammy, brought her presents, sat her on her lap for a bit, then took off again. She did the dirty on JoJo. I reckon he was better off without her although he was ever so upset when he found out. He stuck by her, even when she wanted to get rid of the baby. He's romantic. Men are, usually. They're more romantic than women.'

He smiled at her. From what he had been told, both mother and son considered money pretty romantic. 'Did you know Dominic Merrell?' he asked.

'Not really. I only met him once. He came here with Lisa. He fixed my tap for me. Nice bloke but not half as

113

handsome as my JoJo. You could see she had him under her thumb. Tell you what, Mr Eastwood left me a few of Lisa's things for Tammy. I had a look through the box and there was something of Dominic's in there, from a newspaper. Well, it has his name on the top so it must have been his. It's about some old murder so I don't have any use for it. Do you want it?'

A tingle of anticipation. 'I'd like to take a look.'

She went to a cardboard box in the kitchen and produced a photocopy of a newspaper front page. It was a tabloid paper called *The Lincoln Leader*, dated 14 May, 1979. The headline read *Tragedy of Vietnam Vet and Lincoln Woman*. Swift was about to read on when the front door opened and a child ran down the hallway, holding a carrier bag. He folded the page and put it in his pocket.

'I've got a princess costume, Cora! Look!'

She was tall for her age and had her mother's curls and smile. She was dressed in a gauzy pink smock with gold and pink frills and bows and black patent boots. A plastic silver and pink tiara was in her hair and she was wearing pink nail varnish and sparkling stars on her eyelids. Swift thought she already looked like a mini, low budget princess. She saw him and turned to her father, who was following her in.

'There's a man here,' she said, pointing.

Swift stood. 'Hallo, Tamsin. I came to talk to your grandmother and your dad.'

'Oh, okay,' she said, sitting on the floor and opening her bag.

JoJo Hayworth nodded from the doorway. 'Let's go in the other room.'

'Do you want coffee, my love?' his mother asked.

'No, we're fine. I've got to go soon.'

He was almost as tall as Swift with thick, tousled platinum blond hair. He was as beautiful as his dead wife. He wore black jeans with a white vest under a grey herringbone jacket and navy leather brogues. A trim beard outlined his chin. He looked like the kind of man who stares insolently from the pages of colour supplements. He gazed confidently at Swift as they sat in the tiny front room, which was decorated with many more butterflies, a cuckoo clock and a boldly patterned red carpet. They each sat on a chintz-covered sofa. It was a small space and two tall men made it feel claustrophobic. Their knees almost touched and Swift angled his body to create more room. The heavy curtains blocked the light and you could hear the conversation of passers-by, the calls of children and an idling car engine. Hayworth looked incongruous in the setting, as if he might be taking part in a fashion shoot using a back-street terraced home as an ironic statement.

'I'm sorry about your wife,' Swift said. 'As I explained in my messages, I'm looking into whether or not Dominic Merrell did kill her. Have you any views on that?'

'Why should I? He said he did it. It would seem odd to hang yourself over a crime you didn't commit.' His voice was low, his tone genial and firm. He sat assertively with his arms stretched out along the back of the sofa, legs crossed.

'Most people I've spoken to have said they can't believe it of him.'

He waved a hand. 'I didn't know him. I met him twice at most, briefly.'

'Were you at the party Lisa held the night she died?'

'I didn't attend my wife's parties after we separated.'

'Were you in London?'

'If you're trying to check if I might have popped in on the off-chance and knifed Lisa, the answer is no. I was in Ibiza, being photographed in beach wear.'

'I believe she cheated on you with someone called Richard or Ricardo.'

His arms stiffened slightly. 'You believe correctly. It was the reason why we split up.'

'How did you feel about that?'

'Angry, sad, disappointed. The usual feelings. Time passed, I got over them. What has this got to do with my wife's death?' His manner remained cordial but it was hard to tell if he was sincere.

'It's just part of getting a picture of her.'

Hayworth uncrossed his legs and re-crossed them, glancing at his watch. 'I've only another ten minutes max.'

'I understand you used to like gambling and Lisa funded you.'

'I've gambled some in my time.'

'What kind?'

'Casinos.'

'Enough to argue over it?'

'I don't know what you mean.'

'Someone told me that you visited Lisa just after New Year and you had an argument. She was very upset.'

'Did they? Well, people gossip.'

'She was in trouble financially. Her business was having problems. She wanted money from you, payback for what she'd handed over when you were together.'

'It doesn't surprise me to hear that Lisa had money troubles. She liked to spend. She was always maxed out on her credit cards. It was a bone of contention between us when we were together.'

'Did Lisa give you money when you parted company?'

'I suppose someone has told you that too.'

He smiled. He was pleased with himself. His arrogance was like a third person in the room. The marriage with Lisa must have been lively, two people who liked to get their own way. Hayworth displayed an inflexibility that suggested he could have withstood his wife's appeals.

Swift left a silence, long enough to make Hayworth blink a few times. 'You haven't answered me about the row or the money.'

'Were they questions? We might have had a few words, probably about Tamsin. Yes, that was it. I thought

Lisa should see her more often and she didn't like that. My finances are my business.' The geniality had faded, replaced by curtness.

'And your finances stand to increase with your wife's death.'

'Her father told me she hadn't made a will. Typical Lisa, always *mañana*. Worked in my favour, ultimately. I'm not sure she'd be happy to think I'm getting a chunk of her property, but there we go.' He picked at a manicured fingernail.

'I wouldn't count your chickens about that if I were you.'

'What do you mean?'

'Her business, Body Balm, was in financial trouble and now it's being sued by a customer who was injured. I think Lisa might have mentioned that to you when you had the row. If damages are awarded, a court might look at the property. I don't know but I imagine it's a possibility.'

Hayworth pursed his lips. He looked displeased. 'I'll ask my lawyer about that.'

'Is your career still in modelling? I haven't heard of you.'

Hayworth looked him up and down. 'Well, you don't look as if you take much interest in style or fashion so I'm not surprised. I am a model, yes, busy with work. In demand.'

'Oh? With any big names or just catalogue stuff?' There was a real pleasure in needling the man.

A hint of a frown. 'As I said, I'm in demand.'

'Where do you live now?'

'In London. Although I don't see why that is any of your concern. I have to get going. I'll see you out before I say goodbye to my daughter.'

'You mentioned that Lisa didn't see enough of Tamsin, but your mother says *you* don't visit often.'

Hayworth stood and laughed, hands on hips. 'I'm sure you said you're a private detective, not social services in disguise.' He gestured around. 'Butterfly world. Too much for me, I'm afraid. It only seems charming when you are very young. Once I'm sorted I'll bring Tamsin to London.'

'That your car?' On the doorstep, Swift pointed to the new blue Jaguar F-type coupé parked outside the house.

'It is.'

'Tasty.'

Hayworth shut the door a little too firmly. Swift moved his car down the road and sat in it, keeping an eye on the house. He googled JoJo Hayworth and saw that he had modelled leather bags, beach wear, business suits and fitness clothing in magazines, hair products on billboards, had various bit parts in TV commercials and worked as a film extra. Not exactly the high life, yet he seemed to be in the money. That must be over £50K worth of Jaguar.

Once Hayworth had accelerated away, Swift went back to the house.

'Sorry to disturb you again,' he said to Cora. 'JoJo said he'd give me his address but I forgot to take it. Could you give it to me?'

'Right, my love. Hang on a minute.'

Tamsin appeared in the hall, wearing her new princess costume. It was floor-length, in pale green satin with a pink lace cape and train and silver and gold beading. A green and gold crown sat on her curls.

'Do I look pretty?' she asked, twirling in front of him in pink and green ballet slippers with all her father's self-assurance.

'Lovely. That's a beautiful dress.'

'I know.'

She glided away as her grandmother came back out with a slip of paper, saying that Tammy was all excited now, it would be hell getting her to bed tonight. He glanced and saw that Hayworth lived in Barnes.

Swift decided to drive the few miles to Whitstable and take a look at the sea. He bought a hot falafel wrap and ate it sitting on a bench at the harbour, breathing in the scents of mud, fresh salt air and the incoming tide. The waves were a metallic silver under the grey sky and boat masts were whistling and slapping in the brisk breeze. There were few people about and fat, predatory sea gulls zoomed and screamed.

He felt a rush of adrenalin as he took out the page of newspaper and read through the article which featured a Dominic, but not the man who had partnered Lisa. What he learned confirmed one of his suspicions:

Police have confirmed details of the dreadful tragedy that took place last Saturday in Wakes Avenue, Lincoln. Dominic T. Hill, an American citizen and veteran of the Vietnam War stabbed his girlfriend Judy Chernin, a local woman, with a kitchen knife. He then hanged himself in the bathroom of their first floor flat. Neighbours reported hearing an argument in the early hours of the morning. The next-door neighbour, Mrs Grace Binyon, told our reporter that the couple often had arguments. Mr Hill is thought to have suffered with his nerves following his service in Vietnam. He had left the US air force after a posting in Cambridgeshire, where he met Judy at a dance at the base. A friend said that he had been invalided out of the service although the USAF would not comment on this.

Neighbours were alerted to the tragedy when they heard the couple's two-year-old son crying persistently. Police were called and discovered the bodies. The little boy, also called Dominic, is now in care of social services.

Swift stared out at the rushing tide, and then walked along the pebble beach, over the groynes and past the Lifeboat station. Dominic Merrell had decided to search for his birth parents and had discovered this tragedy. The two-year-old child must have seen his dead parents, might have witnessed the stabbing and his father putting a noose around his neck. He could have been looking at them for hours, calling and crying to them, perhaps trying to wake them up before neighbours intervened. His distress then

119

and now was unimaginable. Did this mean that the adult Merrell had been so traumatised by what he found out that he had suffered a breakdown and been moved to re-enact it? It would make a strange and terrible kind of sense, given all the troubles piling on top of him. Swift turned the thought over but as he watched a gull spearing the water, he was not convinced that things were that clear-cut.

CHAPTER 9

It was late by the time Swift garaged Cedric's car and made for home. He was still thinking about Merrell. Years back, he had dealt with a similar scenario in the Met. He knew that a child who experienced that kind of early trauma could be affected throughout their life.

As he turned off the main road into a deserted side street, he heard high, persistent screams. He quickened his pace and saw a man in the distance. It looked as if he was trying to force someone into a car. Swift started running and shouting. As he drew nearer, he saw Yana twisting and turning in the man's hands, her screams muffled now as he clamped a hand over her mouth. Swift kicked the man hard in the legs and seized his elbow as he grunted and turned, aiming for an arm lock. Yana broke free. 'Run!' Swift shouted and she took off. Her attacker wriggled away and punched Swift hard in the stomach and face, sending him reeling backwards. He managed to catch hold of a lamppost and reached into his pocket for his keys. As the man came for him, he stabbed into his face several times and the attacker staggered, letting out a bellow of pain. Swift balanced, panting. The car door slammed, someone was running and he was hit from behind with a heavy metal object in the back of the legs. As he fell down hard on the pavement, a boot connected with his kidneys. A man yelled, the car doors slammed again. He rolled away and heard the car engine roaring. He managed to lift his head and look at the license plate as it sped off.

He sat up slowly, pain shooting along his back. Breathing was difficult and he could feel blood flowing from his nose. A woman had run from her front door. She was wearing a dressing gown that billowed out as she bent down to him.

'Are you okay? There were two men. I saw them from my bedroom window. Was it a mugging?'

He rolled sideways onto his knees, and then used his hands to push himself upright.

'I'm all right, thanks. Have you got a tissue?'

She pulled one from her dressing gown pocket. 'I'll call an ambulance,' she said.

'No, really, there's no need. I live nearby. I'd rather get home.' He wanted to check that Yana had made it back to Cedric's and was not still on the streets. The car might cruise around looking for her.

'But are you sure?'

'Yes, really. Thanks for your help.'

His legs felt like jelly. He walked away gingerly, aware of the woman standing and watching him. He paused to put the license plate number in his phone, then held the tissue to his nose with one hand and pressed the other hand to his chest, reckoning he had at least one cracked rib.

When he knocked on Cedric's door he could hear the music of a TV late night news programme. Cedric was wearing pyjamas, the gaily-patterned type that he liked. He stared at Swift and pulled him inside.

'Is Yana here?' Swift asked.

'No. I was just starting to worry about her . . . but what's happened to you? Your face is covered with blood.'

'Yana was attacked by a couple of men. I'm going back out to find her if I can. Whereabouts did you say she was sleeping?'

'Past the bridge and along the river path towards Putney. There is that little semi-circular clump of bushes with a bench in the middle. But, Ty, your nose . . .'

'It can wait. Phone me if she comes back.'

'Here.' Cedric pushed a bunch of tissues into his hand and took the blood soaked one he had been pressing to his nostrils.

Swift walked to the river, taking shallow breaths through his mouth. The backs of his legs had started to tingle, the numbness of the blow abating. He stopped by a bin, checking that his nose had dried up and threw the tissues in. A thin sliver of crescent moon hung in the sky. The water was dark and silent, the path deserted. A light, stinging rain started as he approached the bushes to his left. He slowed down. The bench was empty but he thought he had seen a shadow.

'Yana,' he called softly. 'It's me, Ty. Cedric's friend. The men have gone. It's safe now.'

He waited. One of the bushes rustled and she emerged. She stood, watching him.

'They hurt you?' she asked.

'A bit. You?'

'He pull some hair out, hurt my arm.'

'Are they the men who made you work for them in Bolton?'

'Some of them, yes.'

'I need to talk to you but first, do they know where you're staying?'

'I don't think so. I not tell anyone. Honest, I don't.'

She was afraid. 'Okay. Come on, let's go back. You're safer inside.'

He phoned Cedric to tell him. Yana walked back beside him, looking around her all the way. They didn't speak. There were tears of relief in Cedric's eyes when he saw them. He placed a hand gently on Yana's head.

'Come in, come in. I have the kettle on. Ty, wash your face, dear boy, you look as if you have been mauled by a bear.'

Swift washed and examined his swollen nose. He opened his shirt and saw that he had a large bruise just above his stomach. He asked Cedric for an ice pack and some painkillers. Yana had a red mark around her wrist and a bald patch at the back of her head. Cedric gave her arnica cream to soothe her skin. She sat on the sofa, rolling her flute against her cheek.

'Thank you. I am sorry. Your son is right. I bring trouble again. Trouble follows me.'

Swift took a bag of peas from Cedric and held it against his chest. He swallowed painkillers with scalding coffee laced with rum, while Yana and Cedric had cocoa.

'Take your antibiotic. You must finish them,' Cedric reminded her. 'Chest infection,' he explained to Swift. 'The doctor did various tests and we'll go back in a week or so.'

'Good.' Swift was feeling exhausted. Talking hurt. There were pains in his legs, chest, back and face. He drank more coffee and turned the peas. 'The men who attacked us were from Bolton. Yana, how did they know where to find you?'

She pressed the heels of her hands into her eyes. 'I'm sorry,' she whispered.

'I know. You need to tell us. Did you contact someone?'

She nodded and looked at Cedric.

'It's all right, my dear. *You* have done no wrong. Tell us about it.'

'I send email to a girl there, my friend,' she whispered. 'I try, not know if she will get it. She has taken a phone from a man who visit the house, from his pocket while he sleep. So she read it. I tell her if she can get away, I am in London. I tell her I will wait by kebab shop every night at nine o'clock. They must have found out. Do bad things to her.'

'But why come all the way to London for you?' Cedric asked.

Yana picked at her lip. 'I see very bad things there. They worry I tell people.'

This from a girl who must have seen such terrible things in Syria, Swift thought. 'But you definitely didn't tell your friend about this house?'

'I not stupid,' she said with a touch of healthy defiance, rubbing her wrist.

'I think we should call it a night,' Swift said. 'We can talk tomorrow. You need to stay in for now, Yana. No going out. Those men may try again.'

At the door, he spoke quietly to Cedric. 'We need to get Yana to speak to the police. Can you try talking to her tomorrow? She trusts you. I'm going to contact a friend in the Met in the meantime.'

He had eased into bed with an ice pack on his nose and a fresh one against his chest when his phone rang. Nearly one in the morning and an unknown caller. He moved the ice to the side of his face.

'Yes?'

'That Tyrone Swift?' A muffled, nasal voice.

'Yes, who is this?'

'Harry Merrell.'

'Hallo, Harry.'

'Hmm. Thing is, I think I need to talk to ya.'

'Okay.'

'So, my dad . . . my dad . . .' There was a gulping sound, as if he were crying.

'What about your dad?' Swift asked gently.

'Oh God, this is all a mess, all a bloody mess, izzinit?'

'Are you drunk, Harry?'

'S'pose. Yeah. That night, y'know, you were right . . . I was there . . . y'know . . . on my scooter.' His voice dropped as though he was in a tunnel. 'I think my dad . . .

my dad saw me. He must have thought . . . bloody fucking mess.'

'Did you kill Lisa?'

A high-pitched laugh. 'No! But there's somethin' else . . . See, I had to go and help her . . .'

'Help who?'

The voice became indistinct and all Swift could hear was 'ess.' It could have been Lisa.

'I can't hear you, Harry.'

'Yeah, bit sick now, too much to drink. Gotta go.'

'Harry, I'll ring you tomorrow, okay?'

'Nah, I'm away . . . with school. Ring ya when I gebback . . .'

'Okay. Take it easy.'

'Yeah, I s'pose . . .'

The line went dead. Swift lay back, wincing. Someone as taut as Harry had to crack sometime. But what was he cracking about? He recalled the confusion and anger he had felt when his mother died, how he had refused to let his father console him. It had been a time of pain and rage. He had rowed, weeping, the wind stinging his salty eyes. Sometimes he felt that he had never recovered from that loss and never would. The world had been out of kilter ever since and he had mis-stepped through it.

He pulled a pillow against his ribs and fell into an exhausted but fitful sleep, waking every time he moved.

* * *

In the morning, he drank coffee and took more painkillers before stepping into the shower. His nose was dark and swollen and he moved like an old man. He made porridge, and then sat on the sofa with an ice pack against his chest. He emailed Nora, asking if she could look up a license plate and briefly explaining the situation with Yana and the attack:

Would you be willing to call round and see Yana on an informal basis, explain that the police could offer her and the other girls in Bolton protection? I think it would be good if a woman talked to her.

He eased himself up and fetched more coffee, then rang Georgie Merrell. She sounded terse.

'You said you have Dominic's possessions from the flat?' he asked.

'Yes, the police gave some to me and I had the rest of them brought over. I've been through them, sorted out the clothes.'

'Were there papers? Documents?'

'There were some insurance documents, his passport, and a few letters about bills. Why are you asking?'

'I've clarified that Dominic was adopted. I am sure he must have had some paperwork. I'll check with Lisa's father, in case any of his things were mixed in with hers.'

She sighed. 'You think you know someone, and yet he never told me something so fundamental about his life.'

'I don't know when he found out about the adoption. He might not have been hiding it from you when you were together.'

'Who knows? He was certainly good at hiding other things from me, and landing me with surprises.'

It was the first time Swift had heard bitterness in her voice. 'Are you okay?'

'Not really. I've had some correspondence from banks about loans and credit cards, looking for payment of money Dominic owed.'

'How much?'

'Almost twenty thousand pounds — so far. I hope there isn't more I don't know about. I suspect there might be. I am his next of kin and executor, so I have to deal with it. He left no savings so I'm going to have to find the money, possibly extend the mortgage.'

'I am sorry.'

'Yes. In all the time we were together, we were never in debt. Dominic was prudent with money. That woman changed him utterly. It's all such a mess.'

He wondered if he should have told her about her husband's borrowing and theft, his aspirational spending. She was right: this was a horrible situation. Merrell had abandoned her, and then left her his wreckage to deal with. She would have done better to divorce him and not retain any responsibility for his affairs. Swift wondered if this had crossed her mind.

'If you talk to the businesses involved, they might be willing to accept gradual payments. It would be worth taking advice. There are agencies who advise about debt.'

'No. I want it gone, the slate wiped clean. I will just have to bite the bullet and contact my bank. If Dom was here I'd shake him till his teeth rattled.'

Maybe it was good that she was getting angry. 'Is Harry away at the moment? He phoned me last night.'

'He's in Wales on a field trip as far as I know. What did he want?'

'Just to talk. When is he back?'

She laughed. 'How would I know? It's like living with a secret agent. He went on Monday and those trips are usually a few days. That's a bit rich, wanting to talk to you when he blanks me.'

'It's often the way with teenagers though, isn't it? Punishing people they love because they're struggling.'

He ended the call, feeling sorry for her. He didn't yet know how Harry was connected to Lisa's death, but there was a link. His mother would have to know about it at some point. Her burdens were growing.

Swift stayed standing because it was the least painful position to adopt. He wondered where to try next about Merrell's adoption. He knew that getting information from an adoption agency or local council would be almost impossible and guarded by data protection. His phone rang — Georgie Merrell again.

'I was thinking about your call and I remembered that I did give a few things of Dominic's to Finbar Power, some books on fishing mainly. To be honest, I was in such a state I'm not sure exactly what was in the bag I gave him.'

'Thanks. I'll try him.'

He called Power, who confirmed that he had a bag that Georgie had given him. It contained books but he had not sorted through it yet. Swift arranged to visit later in the afternoon. He walked carefully upstairs and checked that Cedric and Yana were all right. She was practising her flute while Cedric completed the crossword. When she saw Swift's nose she said again how sorry she was. He lied, saying it looked worse than it felt. When he told her he had a friend in the police, a woman who might talk to her informally, she looked scared. Cedric reassured her, saying that no harm was going to come to her and she nodded, albeit reluctantly. Swift accepted her invitation to dinner later on.

'I make myself useful, earn my keep,' Yana said. 'I must do something if I not go out, or I go crazy.'

* * *

The towpath around Aurora Dawn was busy but Swift couldn't see any customers waiting for therapy with Body Balm. He could hear raised voices in the cabin as he stepped on board. He knocked on the closed door. Isabella opened it.

'Gosh! What's happened to you?'

'An argument. Can I have a word?'

'Well, Perry and I were just having a meeting . . .'

'Good, because I would like to talk to both of you.'

He stepped through the door. Her kittenish smile wasn't in play as she introduced him to the man he had seen on deck during his previous visit.

'This is Perry Wellings. We work together. Perry, this is the private detective paid by Georgie Merrell.' She sat down, legs akimbo, soles of her bare feet together.

Swift refused a chair and propped himself against the massage table. The air was pungent with lavender again. Wellings was wearing white shorts and T-shirt and deck shoes. His sturdy legs and arms were covered in thick hair, contrasting with the thinning mousy curls on his head. His nose and mouth were too large for his face and his skin was putty-coloured but he had a certain physicality that was attractive. Lisa had certainly gone for different types.

'I'm looking into Lisa's death,' Swift said. 'Since I met you, Isabella, I've talked to Donald Eastwood. He's alarmed about this business, says it hasn't been doing well and you're being sued by a customer who was injured.'

Isabella screwed up her nose. 'That's all being dealt with. People complain, it doesn't mean anything.'

'Surely being sued must mean something? Did Lisa know about this situation?'

'Yeah. She was as pissed off as us.'

'So what happened? How was this customer injured?'

Isabella and Wellings exchanged glances. He fiddled with an earlobe and replied.

'The woman concerned was injured during cupping.'

'That's when heated cups are applied to the skin?'

'That's right. It can be very effective for relaxing muscles and relieving pain,' Wellings confirmed.

'Except in this case it caused it?'

Wellings coughed. His Adam's apple worked up and down. 'The customer had some burns on her back.'

'Look, what's this got to do with Lisa dying?' Isabella asked, folding her arms and frowning. Her previous bounce had gone and her fingernail varnish was chipped.

'I don't know. Nothing, possibly.'

She opened her mouth but didn't speak. Wellings looked up at the ceiling.

'Who did the cupping?' Swift asked, wincing as he moved and a rib complained. After a silence he added, 'you might as well tell me. I can ask Mr Eastwood.'

Wellings spoke. 'My daughter did the cupping.'

'Ah. Is she qualified for that?'

Wellings went to reply, but Isabella cut across him.

'Look,' she said, 'I was off sick that day and Cressida was here so she stepped in when Perry got delayed in traffic. She had seen it done and had the treatment done on her here. And no, she's not qualified.'

Swift thought they might have to part with a lot of money in court or as an out-of-court settlement. 'The business might not survive this?'

'We don't know. Eastwood's talking about winding it up anyway.'

'Someone I've spoken to told me that Lisa had already been talking to you about closing the business. There was a disagreement between you, I was told. With you, Isabella.'

She tutted. 'We did have some words. It got a bit heated. I thought Lisa was reacting too quickly, trying to call the shots. I mean, it was worth seeing if there was a solution — you know, an out-of-court settlement or whatever. This is my living, this business. It's all I have. I haven't got a rich daddy to bail me out whenever I'm in trouble.'

She cast a spiteful glance at him. He looked at her small but capable hands. You did not have to be strong to knife a drunk, sleeping woman.

'You didn't mention this before. It's important.'

'To me. I don't see why it is to you.' She pressed her lips together in anger. 'Anyway, Lisa came back after that and said she'd had a think and she was going to get money off JoJo, quite a bit that she'd loaned him over the years, and she'd put it into the business. She seemed pretty sure he'd give it to her, although I wasn't that optimistic.'

Swift thought about his previous visit to the boat and turned to Wellings. 'Was that your daughter on deck when I was here before, the girl with red hair?'

'That's Cressie.'

'Does she know Harry Merrell?'

Wellings nodded. 'I, ahm, I was with Lisa for a while. Harry came here with her one day after she met Dominic and he and Cressie got friendly.'

'You moved in with Lisa, didn't you?'

'A while ago. It didn't work out.'

'You went back to your wife?'

Wellings nodded, pulling a wry smile. 'I did but then she left me. Said she couldn't trust me. So I'm on my own now.'

'Does your daughter live with her mother?'

'No. She has a place with friends in Barnes somewhere. She's doing really well for herself, she's in international sales.'

Swift stared at the man. He was suddenly aware of his heart pumping as he heard of these connections and the location. Wellings looked proud when he spoke of his daughter, his shoulders lifted.

'Does Cressida know JoJo Hayworth?'

'JoJo was married to Lisa. I don't think so, Cressie's never mentioned him to me.'

'So let me get the order right here. You came after JoJo and Richard but before Dominic?'

Wellings didn't bat an eyelid. 'That's right. Lisa didn't hang about, she got together with Dominic a couple of weeks after I went back home.'

'You didn't get back with Lisa after your wife left you?'

'No, that was all over.' His gaze glanced off Swift at the lie.

'You were at the party the night she died?'

'For a while. It got a bit too loud for me.'

'What time did you leave?'

'I'm not sure. In the early hours.'

'Does either of you own a scooter or a motorbike?'

They shook their heads. Swift left them and walked to a café by the canal where he ordered coffee and a toasted sandwich. He took more painkillers and thought about the two victims whose pasts he had been chasing. His head felt muddled and crowded. He closed his eyes and concentrated. He felt now that he knew both Lisa and Merrell, Lisa more so but that was because she had been flamboyant and people had much more to say about her. Merrell was *quiet, nice, kind*. Swift did not believe he had stabbed his partner. Lisa blew like a gale through people's lives and she had crossed someone and angered them enough to make them take a knife and plunge it into her. Isabella, Wellings or Hayworth were all likely candidates. He had an idea as to why Merrell had confessed, but not enough to support it. He needed to know what Harry had to tell him and to get to Finbar Power. He stood, dizzy for a moment and wincing, taking some careful breaths and bending his knees to ease his leg muscles.

CHAPTER 10

Finbar Power's shop was closed when Swift arrived at half past three. Power answered the bell after a couple of minutes, saying he had been having a siesta. He was shoeless and crumpled, his shirt outside his jeans. He seemed half-awake. He offered Swift an ice pack when he explained his injuries, which he gratefully accepted. Power then vanished and came back with more of the delicious black tea. He brought out a large carrier bag from a cupboard. They sat again by the French window. Power had put on a clean shirt and smelled of minty toothpaste. He looked thinner and there was perspiration on his brow. He dabbed at his forehead with a tissue.

'Are you feeling okay?' Swift asked.

'Can't seem to shake this virus, it keeps coming back. GP thought it could be glandular fever but I tested negative. She finally said there's a lot of it about. I probably ought to take it easy for a couple of days but I have the shop to run. I felt done in this afternoon so I closed up for a while.' He hefted the carrier bag on to his lap. 'I can't believe that Dom didn't tell me about being adopted,' he said. 'There was never any hint of it, in all that time I knew him and his parents. It was their private business but I feel sort of betrayed, although I know that's foolish.'

'That's how Georgie feels. I suppose it seems as if the person's identity has been altered. Dominic must have found it a thorny issue and of course, it may be that he only discovered that he had been adopted after his parents died. Is it okay if I take these things out and look through?'

'Of course. Maybe if you look, then pass to me. I feel bad that I haven't already sorted them out, put them up on the shelves. I had a brief glance and they seemed to be books on fishing. Probably some that I gave Dom over the years. I went to deal with them a couple of times but couldn't bring myself to open them. Something about the finality of it. I miss him.'

'Yes. Grief is hard. People thought well of Dominic and speak well of him. But I think he was travelling without a map.'

Power sipped his tea thoughtfully, a faraway look in his eyes. He cradled his cup, yawning now and again. Swift emptied the carrier bag and placed the contents carefully in a pile on the coffee table. There were half a dozen books and a thin cardboard file. He opened the file first. Inside were photographs of a school sports day, a party in a garden and a couple of a young Merrell and Power fishing by a river. He passed them to Power who looked at them and nodded.

'That was our school sports day. I was pretty good at the long jump and Dom was a sprinter. The party was for my dad's fortieth and that's Dom and me by the river Welland. We caught dace and perch mainly. We would spend all day under the trees, rain or shine. I have no idea what we talked about but we chatted away and the hours vanished. Dom's mum always made us cheese and pickle sandwiches and slices of her sponge cake. Food has never tasted better. She took these photos one day when she came to give us a lift home.' He moved his fingers gently across one of the images, tracing the line of a fishing rod.

The books were all hardbacks and about fishing. A history of fly-fishing, one about sea angling, another on carp and several general guides. Swift riffled the pages of each one. As he flicked through the thickest, an all-purpose guide, he noticed folded paper and a small rectangular envelope taped behind the back dustcover. He drew them out. The pages were a photocopy of an official document, written on a typewriter and headed Lincolnshire Social Services Adoption Team. He pressed them flat on the table and read while Power watched him silently. They were numbered 27 and 28.

Adoption Report for Dominic Paul Hill, DOB 20/3/1977
Summary

Dominic Hill was taken into the care of Lincolnshire social services in May 1979 after the deaths of his parents. He was then aged two. His father, Dominic T. Hill, murdered his mother, Judy Chernin. His father then committed suicide by hanging. He had been receiving treatment for severe depression and was subject to flashbacks to his time in the US forces in Vietnam. (See also coroner's report and attachments.) Mr Hill had previously had an admission to a psychiatric unit where he had responded to treatment but was on daily medication.

Dominic was hungry and distressed when he was brought into care but he had clearly been loved and well cared for before this tragic incident.

Ms Chernin was the only child of Hungarian parents who settled in the UK after the Second World War. They are both deceased. Mr Hill was an American citizen from Missouri with no family in the UK. His parents are also deceased. Extended family in Missouri were contacted but none felt that they could offer a home to Dominic.

Dominic was placed in foster care within weeks of his parents' deaths, with Mr and Mrs Merrell of Stamford, Lincolnshire. Fortunately, he appeared to have little memory of the events that had taken place and settled well with the Merrells. He referred to his birth parents occasionally during the first months and cried for his mother. The Merrells reassured and comforted him and Dominic ceased to mention his previous life. They reported the occasional nightmare and bed-wetting but these gradually abated and Dominic thrived in this placement.

Mr and Mrs Merrell cannot have children. They joined the fostering register with a view to adopting when an appropriate match could be made with a child. They had expressed the wish to adopt a baby but have always understood that this would be difficult. They bonded quickly with Dominic and have worked well to establish a loving and settled home life for him.

Dominic is now almost four years of age and is a contented little boy. He attends nursery school where he has integrated well. He is clearly happy with the Merrells and calls them Mummy and Daddy. They wish to adopt him and can provide a secure and loving environment for him. Mr and Mrs Merrell cooperated fully with the adoption assessment process and demonstrated that they are fully capable and willing to offer Dominic a life with them.

We are therefore applying to the court for an adoption order to be made for Dominic Hill to remain with Mr and Mrs Merrell and recommend that the court accept this application.

Frances Neeley, social worker.
15/2/1981

There was an official stamp at the bottom of the report — Adopt Care, Lincoln, with a phone number and the name Emily de Carolis. It was dated last December.

Swift passed the papers in silence to Power and opened the envelope. Inside was a sheet of blue paper, an original handwritten note in black biro.

The doc says it's good to write things down. She says it might help the constant reliving of memories of Nam. I don't know. I don't think anything can help me or any of the others like me. Like I tell them, I went there to defend my country. I didn't know what it would be like. The heat. I remember the heat. Like I was frying in hell, even in the shade. The heat weighed you down, suffocated you. My skin itched all the time. We were drenched in water and sweat. The leeches and fire ants drove you mad. After a couple of months everyone was nuts. A lot of us took stuff — morphine, heroin, marijuana. I got hooked on morphine. Just to make it all disappear for a while. It's hard to care about anything now. I never sleep for more than a couple of hours. The dreams come, full of fire and heat and screams. I'm angry all the time. I survived two ambushes. Don't ask me how or why. Death became a close friend there and now I feel that he lives with me, walks with me every day. I'm always looking out for him. I'm worried I'll invite him in just to stop the pictures under my eyelids. I got exposed to Agent Orange so I'll probably die of something awful soon anyway. Sometimes I think that's what I deserve. Everyone there hated us and when we went home lots of people swore at us or ignored us. Demonstrated against us. It was all for nothing. I saw men ripped apart for nothing. I loaded helicopters with the bodies. Mangled, limbless, burned men. I lived in a dark world with no hope, every hour of every day. There was a never-ending nightmare of blood and horror. I can never forget it no matter how many pills they give me or how much they talk to me. People like me can't be fixed. There was a never-ending nightmare of blood and horror and I helped create it. The blood is on my skin and always will be.

Swift handed the note to Power and sat, gazing out of the window. He shivered and his breath caught on an arc of pain from his ribs. He put the ice pack on the table and stood for a moment, taking deep breaths.

'My God,' Power said. 'What Dom must have been going through, finding out this terrible thing. He must have been suffering. And he never said a word. It explains why he seemed so down. Oh my good God, if only I had known . . . why didn't he talk to me?' He was close to tears. His face was ashen, haunted.

Swift sat again, thinking. 'Maybe it was all too much for him to take in. He may have been in a kind of shock, and that can paralyse you. He told Lisa. She knew but she

138

couldn't cope with it. Although I suspect she liked the drama of the story.'

Power drew a box of tissues towards him and dabbed at his forehead again. When he spoke, he sounded angry.

'She would. Drama all the way with Lisa. She never knew when to stop. She was . . . she was an angel and a devil. That's how I've come to think of her.'

'There was another drama, too. She'd had an abortion shortly before she died and it couldn't have been Dominic's baby.'

'An abortion? Ah no, no, surely not, she wouldn't have . . . are you sure?'

'The police informed her father.'

Power sat back, staring ahead. When he spoke, his voice was barely audible.

'I remember Dom telling me he'd had a vasectomy, years ago.' He put his head in his hands. 'This is unbearable. These are terrible events. I wonder if Dom knew about that. The poor, poor man.'

Swift was picturing the scene, piecing it together. With all this playing constantly in his mind, Merrell had come home to find his partner stabbed and lying in blood. As he neared home, he had seen Harry on his scooter. He thought his son had killed Lisa, because he resented her or had become intimate with her and couldn't deal with it. If he knew about the abortion, he might have thought it was his son's child. That explained why he refused to see his family in the days after Lisa's death and turned down Georgie's offer of sanctuary. He simply couldn't face them, knowing what he thought he had witnessed. He had sat in the basement of the Hays hotel, alone and in pain, convinced that he was the cause of these calamities. In order to protect Harry he had replayed a terrible history to its conclusion.

Swift looked at Power. His face was flushed, his chest rising and falling rapidly. The man needed to go to bed.

'If it's okay with you, I need to take these adoption documents and the letter. I imagine Georgie might want to hang on to them in the long run.'

Power nodded listlessly.

'Maybe you should rest up, take it easy. You really look done in. It is a lot to come to terms with. I'm sorry all this has come out, adding to your grief.'

'Never mind me. I'm not important. What about Georgie and the boys? How will they deal with this? It's all such a hopeless mess and I can't do anything to help.'

Swift left Power sitting and gazing at the photograph of two young boys by the river, dressed in waders, holding up their rods proudly for the camera.

* * *

Harry Merrell had eventually replied to two texts from Swift, saying he needed to speak to him: *Back home Friday. Meet you at mine eight p.m.*

Two days' time, it would have to do. He decided that he would speak to Georgie Merrell after he had seen Harry. The harrowing information he had discovered needed a face-to-face discussion. He had showered before going to Cedric's for dinner and was carefully drying himself, avoiding bruises and his battered nose, when Ruth rang. His heart lifted when he heard her but he couldn't help thinking of Williams in the background and wondering if he knew she was calling him.

'You sound funny. Have you got a cold?'

'No. I was in a fight with a pimp. I'm okay.'

'I hope your daughter can't hear this.'

'She'll be educated in it, don't worry. How is she? How are you?'

'All fine. I am looking roly-poly and I have to sleep on my back. Emlyn hasn't been well. He got a chest infection but the antibiotic has kicked in now. He has been notified of a trial date in July. I think it knocked him.'

A barrister appearing in the wrong part of the court. Swift could feel no sympathy and changed the subject abruptly. Ruth was a psychologist and he was hoping she could help. He explained the circumstances of Dominic Merrell's confession, his childhood and adoption.

'The social worker's adoption report stated that he stopped having nightmares and being upset but presumably that kind of traumatic incident could resonate in later life, particularly if he found out details about it?'

'Well, yes, if he discovered information as an adult it could certainly trigger memories. What happened to him at the age of two would be an embedded trauma. That kind of event would have a deep impact, even in such a young child. Children over the age of two form autobiographical memories, even if they don't recall them. Also, at the age of two he would have picked up on the shock of the people around him, those who found him and cared for him. Oh, this poor man. He found out as an adult that neither of his birth parents could keep him safe and that his own father killed his mother. Did he already know he had been adopted?'

'I don't know. I'll try to find out. It looks like a case of the trauma suffered by the father overwhelming the son. I'm becoming convinced that when Merrell found his partner dead, the terrible events he had recently uncovered became real and devastating for him. He started to obsess about them and relate them to the present.' That was why he had repeated the phrase about a nightmare and blood. He had encountered his own Vietnam.

'That's quite possible. He must have had counselling if he was looking for information about his adoption and the records, particularly in such awful circumstances.'

'That would only help so much and it would have been before the murder of his partner. I'd better go, I'm having dinner with Cedric and Yana.'

'The refugee girl?'

'Yes. She has moved in with him temporarily. I'll tell you more later.'

Nora was coming for dinner too, having agreed to speak to Yana. Why hadn't he mentioned her name to Ruth? He was too tired to think about it and his chest was tight. He dressed in jeans and a white shirt, took another painkiller and answered the door to Nora's ring. Her hair was tousled from the breeze and tonight her string bow tie was cream with tiny purple tulips. She smiled at him as she stepped in.

'Love the beat-up nose. Lip kiss or cheek kiss? I'm muddled after the other night.'

He bent down and kissed her lips lightly by way of an answer, groaning as his muscles complained.

'Ribs as well as nose,' he explained.

'All courtesy of this Yana's "friends?"'

'That's right.'

'Ah well, if you will be a knight in shining armour . . . The car license plate you gave me. It was traced to an address in Bolton but the house was cleared out, our birds had flown.'

'Predictable, I suppose.'

* * *

They ate a delicious main meal of fish with spiced rice and caramelised onions, which Yana told them was called *sayadieh*. Her hair was clean and gleaming, black-blue in the light and hung free. Cedric had bought her some new clothes and she was wearing a green and purple woollen tunic with black leggings. She looked like a person with a life and a purpose as she accepted compliments on the meal. Dessert was *Maamoul bi Ajwa*, a crumbly biscuit with date filling which went well with coffee.

Nora chatted easily to her, drawing her out about her life and her journey to England with her brother.

'My mother was music teacher, my father bookkeeper. We had a house, a lovely house. But now I am here.'

'You're amongst friends now, you're safe,' Nora told her.

Her eyes filled and she lowered her face over her cup.

Nora leaned towards her. 'Yana, the police went to the house in Bolton, the house you escaped from. It was empty. The business will have moved elsewhere. There is a search on for the car but they will have got rid of it or hidden it somewhere by now. These men are good at doing this. They are practised in it. Were you taken to any other houses in or around Bolton?'

The girl shook her head. 'Only that one.'

'Have you heard from your friend at all?'

'Nothing.'

'Okay. You told Ty and Cedric you had seen something terrible and that's why those men came after you. Would you be able to talk to me about that?'

'I can't. Don't make me do that.'

'Nobody will make you do anything. If you can talk to the police, we can offer you witness protection. That means we look after you. We can explain it in more detail. You know, if you talk to us we can help your friend and other girls as well.'

Yana shook her head and was silent. Nora looked at Swift and made a little gesture of defeat.

'Okay. But just think it over. Talk to Cedric, yes?'

The girl remained wordless. Cedric poured more coffee.

'Yana chats away to me. We'll see how it goes,' he said. 'I presume in the meantime, it's best if she doesn't go out.'

'Absolutely. I'm sorry this has happened, Yana, after your other troubles.'

Yana looked up. 'But I have friends now. And I have been trapped in places with no friends. It's no punishment to stay inside here as long as Cedric allows.'

'You do have friends,' Swift said. 'Can I ask a favour of you? Would you play your flute for us?'

Relief swept over her face. She fetched her flute and played several fast tunes, then a slower air. Her expression changed as she played, focused and energised.

Nora had to leave them to finish writing a report. Swift saw her out. At the front door, she kissed her finger and placed it against his lips.

'A drink again soon?' she asked.

'Yes, of course.'

'Let me know about the baby.'

'I will.'

She smiled at him. 'Timing . . . what to say?'

He went back to Cedric's to help clear up. Yana was in the bathroom, singing in a light, tuneful voice. A song in her own language.

'She showers three times a day,' Cedric told him. 'Says she can't get clean enough.' He stacked the dishwasher. 'She won't talk to the police, you know. Her life has been full of men in uniforms, corralling her, ordering her, threatening her and she is understandably wary of authorities, however benign they seem. She is sad for the other girls but she is too terrified to talk, at least for now. Terrified and also determined to survive. She's a steely person underneath the apparent fragility, knows her own mind.'

'That's how she's got through. I can't say I blame her. She can't stay with you longer term though, on the sofa.'

'No, I know. Maybe if say a month or so passes and she stays in for that time, I can help her find somewhere. Do you think the danger will be over then?'

'Hard to say. She must have witnessed a serious crime. Keep her in, anyway. She would probably be safe enough then in another part of London.'

He wiped down the work surfaces. Cedric was looking at him as he dried a saucepan.

'Nora seems a very nice woman,' he said. 'Have you known her long?'

'A while,' Swift said distantly. 'Do you want me to put this leftover food in the fridge?'

Cedric knew not to intrude further and started the dishwasher.

CHAPTER 11

Swift was passed through three people at Adopt Care, explaining each time who he was and why he was calling. Each sounded more cautious than the last. A fourth finally confirmed that a care manager called Emily de Carolis had worked for them but had returned to Canada. He was told that a manager would ring him back.

He set off for Barnes in Cedric's car to explore the possible Cressida Wellings/JoJo Hayworth connection. He had no idea if it was relevant to his enquiries but all leads were worth a try. Hayworth's address was a penthouse flat in a newish riverside development called Willow Bank. He parked and looked out at the gleaming river, frustrated because his rib injury would stop him from rowing for at least a couple more days. The early afternoon was bright with high cloud and a fresh wind. Excellent conditions. Ah well.

Swift pressed the bell for number 11 by the intercom but there was no reply. He pressed again and waited. He tried a few more random bells but no one was answering. He returned to the car and was debating whether to hang around when Adopt Care phoned him. A woman introduced herself as Hannah Seaford and asked how she could help. He explained yet again who he was and why he had contacted the agency.

'I see. I have run a few checks on you. You will appreciate that our records are completely confidential. I can confirm that Ms de Carolis met Mr Merrell and gave him information from his file but I can't discuss this with you,' she said. She was quietly spoken, polite but firm.

'I understand, but you see, I don't believe that Dominic Merrell murdered his partner. Papers have been found amongst his belongings, including those given to his wife. I have read the adoption report summary that he received detailing the circumstances of his parents' deaths and the description of Vietnam written by his father. He must have been deeply upset. I think that the impact of knowing about his background contributed to his state of mind and his decision to confess to a crime he hadn't committed.'

'You may be correct. I'm not allowed to give you details.'

Swift thought. 'I appreciate your position. Bear with me a minute, because I really am trying to defend this man and identify a murderer. If . . . if I told you that Dominic Merrell knew he had been adopted but not the dreadful circumstances causing it and decided to look for his birth parents in the last year or so, would I be wrong?'

She cleared her throat. 'Not necessarily.'

'He'd never told his wife or family or close friends that he was adopted. I suppose, generally speaking, that can happen.'

'Generally speaking, that can happen. People can feel ashamed or aware that their adoptive parents would be distressed if they revealed it. Sometimes, being adopted just isn't a huge issue for them or they can think it isn't until something triggers a need to investigate it, usually a major life event. There are many reasons. It's a complex area.'

'And I suppose, generally speaking, that adoptive parents might not reveal previous traumatic events to a child through a wish to protect them.'

'That could be the case.'

'And again, generally speaking, it could be the case that a life event such as a marriage breaking up could be a trigger to seeking information.'

'It could.'

He had spotted Cressida Wellings walking along the road, wearing her coat with the fur collar, talking into her phone. He had to double check because her hair was now the colour of pale honey.

'Okay. Thank you so much. I won't bother you further.'

His head buzzing, Swift watched as Cressida stopped at Willow Bank and entered a code on the keypad by the door. He waited for a few minutes, then walked over and rang the bell again.

'Cressie speaking,' she said softly.

He spoke into the intercom. 'Hi. My name's Tyrone Swift. I'm a private detective. I met you briefly on the Aurora Dawn when I was visiting Isabella Alfaro. You were on deck with your dad. Could I have a word? I have ID.'

A pause. 'How did you know where I live?'

'Oh, JoJo told me. I was talking to him.'

'JoJo?'

'Yes. JoJo Hayworth. I saw him in Canterbury. Could I speak to you?'

Her voice had sharpened. 'It's not really convenient now.'

'Hmm. It's just that I know you're friendly with Harry Merrell and I wanted to check something.'

A longer pause. 'I've got a few minutes. You can come up.'

There was a lift at the end of a gleaming foyer with black-and-white marble tiled flooring and tall, lush pot plants. The lift had a large mirror and he checked his nose as he rode up. He looked only mildly disreputable.

Cressida opened the door, glanced at his ID, looked him up and down and led him into a long living area with huge glass windows offering a panoramic view of the Thames. He felt as if he had walked on to a film set. The place was opulent, with sofas, a chaise longue and chairs in cream leather, thick cream carpet, huge gilt-edged mirrors and several large pieces of metal sculpture. A heavy perfume scented the air. All was light and space and the rippling river reflected the sun, drawing the eye. At one end of the room there was an L-shaped mahogany cabinet, standing open, displaying a home bar stocked with dozens of bottles and a champagne bucket and glasses.

'Amazing place,' he said.

Cressida was standing by the chaise longue, hand on a hip, watchful. She was wearing a short red wraparound dress in a silky material, which exposed a deep cleavage. Her long, muscular legs were in sheer black nylon. She had on red-and-black stilettos. Her hair was brushed out around her shoulders, her lips outlined in a deep, shimmering coral. She presented an interesting picture at one thirty in the afternoon.

'You've changed your hair colour,' he added.

She made an impatient movement with her hand. 'What do you want to speak to me about?'

She hadn't offered a seat so he sat on a plush armchair. She frowned and perched on the edge of the chaise longue, tucking her legs to one side.

'I was talking to your father when I went back to the Aurora Dawn. He doesn't seem to know you live here with JoJo.'

'So?'

'It's a bit odd, that's all.'

'I'm an adult. It's my business who I live with.'

'Sure, but it still seems odd because I understand you are close to your dad. I suppose you must feel bad about the cupping incident at Body Balm and your dad's workplace being sued.'

She flicked her hair and shifted her balance on the seat. 'Why exactly are you here?'

'I'm investigating Lisa Eastwood's death. Dominic Merrell might be innocent.'

'And that brings you here because . . . ?'

'Well, let's see.' He ticked off on his fingers: 'You know Harry Merrell, your dad and Lisa used to be an item and Lisa was married to JoJo. Your accident with a client was the reason Lisa and Isabella argued and why the business is in jeopardy. So you connect people and events in a significant way and that's always of interest to me. Were you at Lisa's party?'

Her eyes narrowed. 'No.'

'Was Harry?'

'How would I know?'

'Your dad was, though.'

'Was he?' She made a little movement with her shoulder and glanced at the huge brass wall clock. She had a pretty but bland face with shapely eyebrows. The peachy bloom on her skin was appealing and he supposed she had a certain sultry attractiveness. She was a cool customer, he thought. Observant.

'He was. Lisa was interested in him again, eyeing him up. Presumably he was responding or he wouldn't have accepted her invitation.'

'I don't monitor my dad or who he's spending time with. He's a grown-up like me, he can do what he likes with his life.' Her voice fell a little, belying her assertion.

'What's your relationship to Harry Merrell?'

'He's a friend.'

'A good friend?'

'Yes.'

'I suppose you've had plenty to discuss. You both had fathers who fell for Lisa, fell foul of her, some might say.

You both experienced family upheaval because of it. It would give you a kind of bond.'

'Would it?' She yawned, showing her soft pink tongue.

'Yes, I think it would.' He gave her a long, steady look. 'I was a teenager once. I tasted grief for the first time when I was fifteen. Huge life events are hard to deal with at any time, but particularly when you are trying to establish your own individuality, find a course in life. Parents who misbehaved and caused heartache would have drawn you and Harry together.'

A tiny vein was twitching in her cheek. She gave another little yawn. 'You're quite the philosopher.'

'Just got some miles on the clock. You know, you remind me of Harry. He is cloaking his confusion in hostility. You're putting on a cool, sophisticated act. It's pretty transparent.'

'If you say so.' She frowned and looked away, as if she were searching for something.

'I've heard that you gave your father grief about his previous liaison with Lisa. You must have been upset about that, particularly as it split your parents up. Despite your nonchalant manner, I think you wouldn't have much liked the idea that he was being tangled in her web again. Daughters can be possessive about their fathers, or so I've heard.'

'Have you? Maybe it is true. But don't believe everything people tell you.'

'How about Lisa and Harry? Was he involved with her?'

She froze and threw him a look of disgust. 'No, he wasn't. Harry's a decent bloke, he wouldn't have behaved like that.'

'I'd agree with you there. But something's eating him up and I think it's more than the two deaths.'

She took a breath. 'I'd love to sit and chew the fat with you about our friendships and our personal affairs but you have to go now, I have an appointment.' She rose in a fluid movement and walked towards the door. Swift watched her dress sway and slide.

'When I talked to JoJo he had an appointment to get to and now you're the same.'

'I suppose we're both busy people.'

'Or evasive. Your dad was very proud of your successful career. What is it you do?'

She pressed her lips together. 'I'm in sales. Good luck with your enquiry.'

There was defiance in her eyes. She watched him walk to the lift before she closed the door softly. He could smell her heavy, resinous scent on his clothes as he went down the stairs to the foyer. He suspected that Cressida was indeed in sales, of the high class, expensive variety and not the sort her father would approve of. There was a small alcove with a bow window by the entrance on the ground floor. He stepped in there, watching the front of the building and practising deep breaths in and out while he waited. His ribs were a little easier. He followed up with gentle calf stretches and a few neck rolls. After five minutes he saw a chauffeur-driven black Bentley draw up outside. The chauffeur, in grey uniform and peak cap, got out and opened the rear nearside door. A well-padded, middle-aged man in a suit exited, looked at his watch and exchanged a few words with the driver, who nodded and doffed his cap.

Swift waited while the man pressed a buzzer and was admitted. Once he was in the lift, Swift ran upstairs to the top floor, holding his chest. The lift door was opening as he arrived. He watched as the man was welcomed to number 11.

The Bentley was still outside, the chauffeur replacing the cap on a water bottle. Swift wandered round to his door and tapped on the window.

'Haven't got a light, have you?' he asked when it glided down.

'Sorry, don't smoke.' He was in his sixties, fit looking, smart, clipped moustache and quick eyes. Ex forces, Swift reckoned.

'Oh okay. Lovely car. I used to be a chauffeur, drove a Mercedes. Worked for a Middle Eastern family. Trips to Harrods, mainly.'

The chauffeur smiled. 'I'm with an agency.'

'Interesting work, I bet. Something new every day.'

'That's right.'

'I think I've seen you here before. I do maintenance.'

'Maybe. I bring a gent here around this time every week.'

'Oh. Business meeting of some kind, I suppose.'

The man tapped his nose. Swift leaned closer.

'That's what he implies, but I sniff a knocking shop.'

'Crumbs! In this place?'

'You'd be surprised. There are quite a few in upmarket addresses like this, dotted all around London. Posh totty for executives and the like — discreet, high class, expensive. If you can afford it . . . out of my budget range plus the wife would kill me. Put it this way, after exactly two hours my gentleman always comes out with a smile on his face and humming a little tune, so I don't think he's visiting his granny.'

'Well, you learn something every day,' Swift said. 'Best get on or I'll get the sack. See you around.'

The chauffeur started the engine and purred away. Swift sat in the car for a while. Cressida was a link of some kind in all of this, but she had to be a suspect too. If she had thought that her father was seriously thinking of returning to Lisa she might have been angry enough to pick up a knife. He had glimpsed a deep unease. Something was eating away at her, despite her admirable, practised control. But there was a steely look about her too that made him think he wouldn't want to be on the wrong side of her.

* * *

There was no reply when Swift rang the Merrell's doorbell on Friday evening. It was almost dark and there was a light on in the hall. The curtains were pulled across the front window. He tried the brass knocker on the door with no result. He rang Harry's mobile but it went to answerphone. He looked through the letterbox but there was no sound, no Sid panting or barking. He could smell a faint trace of curry, suggesting that dinner had been eaten. The hallway looked neat with its filled shoe rack, coats on hooks and small wicker table with a bowl for keys.

He walked round to the garage. The door was closed but he tried the handle and it turned. He lifted the door up and was reaching for his pocket torch when someone sprang forward, shoved him forcefully and bolted. He lost his balance and fell against the scooter, banging his right arm and his head. He yelled as his bruised ribs felt the fall. He lay dazed for a few moments, then used the Vespa to right himself and ran out to the street. He didn't know which way his attacker had turned. He chose the right, towards the main road and ran to the top of the street. No sign of anyone. He leaned against a lamppost for a moment, and then ran back to the garage, torch at the ready.

Harry was sitting slumped across his drum kit, his face resting to one side on the cymbals where he had fallen forward, his mouth open. A double-edged bladed knife with a curved handle was sticking out of his back. Swift felt for a pulse but there was no flicker. His beanie hat wouldn't keep him snug now but his skin was still warm. His attacker had struck recently and had probably heard footsteps, delaying an escape. Swift looked for the light switch and used a tissue to turn it on. Blood was sprayed brightly across the drums and on the concrete floor in a random pattern. Its familiar coppery taint was in the air. Swift looked at where the knife had penetrated, knowing it must have pierced a lung and possibly his heart. Harry's hands dangled downwards, with no evidence of defensive wounds. His drumsticks lay on the floor near his feet. It looked as if he would have had no idea that he was in danger. Either he had not heard someone enter the garage behind him or he had known them and had been playing his drums when attacked.

Swift stepped outside and closed the door. He rang emergency services and walked up and down on the pavement, trying Georgie Merrell's mobile. It was switched off and he couldn't leave a message. He felt chilled, shocked. Images of Kris lying dead on the floor played through his mind. Another young person dead, another promising future ended with a knife.

Two police cars arrived. A slim Asian man in a well-cut suit and sparkling white shirt beckoned Swift with a finger while issuing instructions to a subordinate. A uniformed officer set about taping off the road on both sides of the house. Porch lights were switched on as neighbours looked out of their front doors.

'You're Swift? You rang in?' the dapper man asked.

He recognised the curt tone. 'Yes.'

'DCI Kharal, leading this enquiry.'

'Yes, we've spoken before. I'm a private detective, employed by Mrs Merrell.'

Kharal looked as if he had sucked a lemon. 'I'm going to look in the garage. Wait here. Where are the family?'

'I don't know. They're out somewhere.'

He waited while Kharal and a colleague donned protective clothing and went into the garage. Ten minutes later, a forensics team arrived and set up their equipment. Swift glanced in. With floodlights and masked and gowned figures, it looked like a makeshift laboratory. Kharal was staring at the floor, then the knife. He looked up, saw Swift watching and ordered the door to be closed. Swift walked away and leaned against the Merrells' gate. He went back over the brief conversation he'd had with Harry on the phone. He had acknowledged being at Lisa's with his scooter and he thought that his father had seen him. He had gone there because he had to help 'her.' Then he had slurred 'ess.' Swift repeated the word silently, then felt as if a light had beckoned him. He thought of a silky red dress. Not Lisa — Cressida. If Harry knew that Cressida killed Lisa and she had found out he was about to talk to Swift . . . had she stabbed both of them? He thought it possible but somehow it didn't hang together. Why would Harry have stayed quiet for so long?

He needed to go back over the information he had gathered but now a car was coming slowly up the road and parking just beyond the police tape. Georgie, Adam and Sid got out. She looked distracted. A police officer walked towards her. Sid was straining on his leash and Adam looked up at his mother, then at the police officer. Adam picked up the dog and held him tight as his mother fell to her knees on the road, her bag and car keys flying. She began to howl.

Harry's body was taken away at around eleven p.m. Kharal questioned Swift in Georgie's living room, while she and Adam were comforted by officers in the kitchen. Kharal twirled a chair around so that its back faced Swift and sat astride it, looking self-conscious. His eyes were bright in his narrow face. His dark hair was slicked back. His tone was aggressive and cocky, his voice strident. Promoted too fast, knows it and is trying to compensate, Swift thought. He explained that Harry had contacted him, saying he needed to talk and had made an appointment.

'A neighbour of Lisa told me she heard an engine outside in the early hours after the party, around the time Lisa was killed. Harry owns a scooter. He said he was there but he didn't kill her.'

'What? Was he sweet on her or something — like father, like son?'

Kharal was excavating his right ear with the tip of his little finger. Swift rarely took an instant dislike to people but he was prepared to make an exception with Kharal.

'I don't know.'

'Any idea what he wanted to tell you?'

'None.' He decided not to mention Cressida. Kharal could do his own work.

'Why didn't you tell the police about this?'

'You had your confession. I wasn't sure it was important.'

Kharal smoothed his tie between his thumb and forefinger. 'Have your *important* enquiries given you any idea who wanted to stick a knife in young Merrell's back?'

'No.'

'There's something pretty weird going on here. Bloody hell, first the father, now the son! Bad luck or something nastier? Has someone got it in for the whole family?'

'I don't know. There must be a connection.'

'Haven't got very far, have you?'

'Apparently not.'

Kharal registered the provokingly mild tone and looked surly. 'And you didn't see who pushed you?'

'It was dark and he came at me from the dark.'

'He?'

'I think so. Tall, strong, quick on his feet. It could have been a woman but I got the impression it was a man. It was all over in a moment.'

'So, you think the dad was guilty or innocent?'

'Probably innocent. But I'm still working on the details.'

'Who thumped you?'

'Different case, nothing to do with the Merrells. DI Nora Morrow is aware of it if you need to check.'

'So many police buddies,' Kharal snapped.

'Are you pissed-off because you're not one of them or do you just wake up grumpy?'

Kharal stood abruptly, instructing him to attend and make a signed statement the following day. They went through to the kitchen where Kharal told Georgie that until he knew the reason for Harry's death, he was

157

concerned for her and Adam's safety. He asked if she had somewhere she could stay but she insisted dully that she wanted to remain in her own home. Kharal looked annoyed but backed off from pressurising a grieving woman. He said that he would arrange for twenty-four hour protection, with a police car stationed outside the house. Swift offered to stay with Georgie for a while, if she wanted him to. She agreed, saying she would rather the police left her alone if they had finished.

It was well after midnight by the time the door closed behind them. Georgie's eyes were dry but pouched and narrowed, as if her face had been squeezed. Adam was in bed but she said she wanted to check on him. Swift put the kettle on while she went slowly upstairs. The kitchen was orderly, with a small homemade breakfast bar and a couple of stools against one wall. He guessed that Merrell had made it. There were mauve pansies in a pot on the window ledge alongside a little group of pebbles, a glass jar of marbles, a phone charger, a china bell, a black-and-white cat made of plasticine and a brass horseshoe. A cookery book was open on the work surface at a recipe for fish pie. There was a white *to do* board attached to the fridge and beside it a small laminated card:

> *5 Essential Commands for your Dog*
> *Sit*
> *Come*
> *Down*
> *Stay*
> *Leave it*

The calendar on the wall featured Georgie's animal illustrations. He looked at the awful Friday that had just passed and saw, *7pm, Sid for training at community centre.* The dog was not around and Swift guessed that Adam had been allowed to take him to his bedroom. He found a blue-and-white teapot and warmed it with boiling water before putting tea bags in. It was what his father had always done and rituals were a comfort when sorrow came calling. He cupped his hands around the teapot. His chest was throbbing again and he took a couple of painkillers.

Georgie came down and they took their tea into the living room.

'Adam's fast asleep. Sid is curled up beside him. Isn't it strange, how children can be terribly upset but still sleep soundly? I wish we didn't lose that knack as adults.' She looked at him, her face raw and naked. 'My husband, and now my son. What is happening?'

He didn't want to tell her anything that would give her false hope. She was staring into her tea as if she might find answers in the cup. He recalled a woman at police training college who said she had been taught by her great grandmother to read tea leaves. It was the first time he had heard of the art of tasseography. She had a special white china cup, very deep and she would sit in the refectory, reading the leaves for those wishing to know their futures.

'I'm so sorry. What has happened here is terrible. I don't know what the police have told you. Listen to me carefully now. This is hard. Harry asked to meet with me. That is why I came here and found him. He had been near Lisa's flat with his scooter on the morning she died. All I know is that he was there to help someone but I'm not sure who. He believed that his father saw him as he was coming back from work. I think Dominic thought that Harry had stabbed Lisa and that is why he confessed. He wanted to take the blame away from his son.'

She looked at him, frowning. 'That man, Kharal, he said something about Harry and his scooter. I didn't really understand. But Harry . . . Harry didn't kill Lisa, surely?'

'No, I don't believe he did.' He took one of her hands and held it. It felt chilly and lifeless. 'Georgie, I still have work to do but I think Harry and Dominic are innocent victims in all this. I don't know who has done this to Harry or why, but I believe the two murders are linked.'

She shook her head. 'I hadn't seen him for days. He came back at lunchtime yesterday. We exchanged just a few words. I asked him how his trip had been and he shrugged, muttered it had been okay but wet. He threw some dirty laundry in the machine, heated soup in the microwave and went upstairs. I didn't speak to him again. When he was little we chatted all the time. He had such a sense of humour. I used to call him my monkey because he would wind his arms around my neck and his legs about my waist and cling to me.' She put her tea down, untasted.

'What time did you and Adam go out to dog training?'

'Six thirty.'

'Was Harry in then?'

'I think so. He had been playing his drums late afternoon but then it went quiet. I heard him in the bathroom around six, when I was getting changed.'

'It was definitely Harry?'

'Hmm? Oh, yes. Adam was in the garden with Sid, I could see them through the window.'

Swift reached into his pocket and withdrew the adoption papers and Dominic Hill's letter.

'I found these documents in the things you'd given Finbar Power. Dominic had found out some very difficult information. I think he knew he was adopted but not why. I don't know what the Merrells had told him, but it wasn't the truth. This isn't an easy time for you to see this but I think you need to and no time is going to be good.'

He sat and watched her reading. He topped up his tea. It tasted stewed and bitter but he drank it. Hers sat untouched. When she had finished she laid the papers in her lap.

'My poor husband. The more you tell me, the more I feel he was a lost soul. This . . . this previous stabbing and hanging. It's a mirror image of Lisa and Dominic.'

'Exactly. I'm still working out why.'

She leaned forward, chin in her hands, her bony wrists protruding from her jumper. 'There are just the two of us now. Once we were a family, the house was noisy and happy. Now . . . two.'

'Yes. You have had a lot to endure. Do you think you should try and get some rest?'

'What's the point? I won't sleep. I can't make sense of any of this. My poor, poor boy. My poor Harry.'

They sat in silence. After a while, her head fell back and he saw that she was dozing. Now and again her limbs twitched like a marionette's. She looked a hundred years old, her face sagging, the waxy colour of molten candles. He took a yellow patchwork quilt patterned with hares and rabbits from the back of the sofa and laid it over her, turned off the main light and switched a lamp on. He washed up the tea cups, checked that the doors and windows were locked and left her a note in the kitchen saying he would phone her. He closed the front door quietly.

CHAPTER 12

The night was unexpectedly chilly with a full, glowing moon. Swift started walking, having a general idea of his route, thinking, puzzling, trying out ideas as he paced street after street. An empty taxi slowed, looking for business but he shook his head and walked on. His blood flowed and the cold, dry air was invigorating. A sleek, confident fox crossed his path at a junction. It stopped and stared at him, then trotted away. As he entered Fulham, he was reflecting on his last conversation with Isabella Alfaro. Fully alert despite the hour, he stopped for a moment, concentrating on an idea, and then ploughed on. In just under two hours, he opened his front door, knowing what his next move would be.

As he took off his jacket, he had a text from Ruth:

In hospital overnight. Had abdominal pain but they say it's caused by ligaments being stretched. Keeping me here until morning to be on safe side. Just thought I'd let you know. Will ring you when I'm home x

Home with Emlyn, he thought. Perhaps Emlyn was there in the hospital with Ruth now, sitting by her bed, holding her hand. It was all too much to bear and yet it had to be borne. He felt suddenly shattered and aware of the niggling ache in his chest. He poured himself a large whisky, swallowed a couple of strong codeine tablets, and sat on the sofa, texting Ruth. *Okay, thanks for letting me know. Sleep well and speak tomorrow* x

He finished his drink and lay back on the cushions for a moment. At half past four he woke, his neck aching. Cats were fighting in the night, yowling and hissing. One of them started a thin, high wail like a crying baby. It made his scalp prickle. Groggy from the codeine, he stumbled to bed, sinking under the duvet still clothed.

* * *

Swift wanted to get to Cressida before she heard about Harry. If it got him into trouble with Kharal, so be it. He was up at seven, had a shower, groaning under first scalding and then cold water, grabbed a muesli bar and a banana and was parked outside Willow Bank by eight fifteen. He kept his finger on the bell, ringing six times.

'Yes?'

Not Cressida. A woman's voice, sleepy sounding, grumpy.

'I need to speak to Cressida Wellings urgently. My name's Tyrone Swift.'

'Hold on.'

He waited. Several minutes passed. The early light was clear, dappling the water. He watched the tree tops swaying in the breeze and envied a six-woman crew rowing down the river, their oars lifting and dipping in beautiful harmony.

'Cressida speaking.'

'I need to talk to you. It's urgent.'

'It's not convenient. I've nothing to tell you anyway.'

'I have serious news about Harry, that's why I'm here so early. You need to let me in.'

The door clicked open. When he arrived, she was in a short blue satin dressing gown, her hair pulled back in a ponytail. Free of make-up she looked younger, except for her bleary eyes.

She stood in the doorway, blocking entry. 'What is it?'

'I'm not talking here.'

She tapped a bare foot, then stood aside and led him in. The place reeked of alcohol, although the bar was now closed up. She opened a window and ran her fingers under her eyelids.

'Hard night?' Swift asked, sitting down and taking off his jacket.

'Late night.' She sat opposite him. Her dressing gown slid open, revealing a length of thigh. She didn't seem to notice.

'What do you charge?'

'Pardon?'

'If I asked you for an hour of your time, what would you charge? I understand the man who was here yesterday usually has two hours.'

She stared at him and folded her arms. 'I don't know what you're talking about. What's happened to Harry?'

He shook his head at her. The movement hurt from his collision with the scooter. 'You're lying to me. You know exactly what I'm talking about. You lied about the night Lisa died as well. You were at her flat. Harry was there too, with his scooter. He told me about it.'

'He can't have.' She stopped.

'But he did. He told me enough. You can carry on lying but there's no point.'

She put a hand on her lips, and then rallied. 'Harry wouldn't have told you. He's not like that. He promised me.'

'Every time you open your mouth you put your foot in it. You're not as hard and streetwise as you think. The cracks are visible. Harry's father hanged himself and you contributed to his reasons for doing that. You are in deep trouble here, you know. When did you last talk to Harry?'

She sat back. He could see her spinning through her thoughts, trying to gauge how much he knew.

'Yesterday morning. He rang me. He was on his way back from Wales.'

'He told you he was going to talk to me?'

'Yes, but then after we spoke he agreed he wouldn't. I asked him not to and he said okay. What is it about him? Has he had an accident?'

'He's dead.'

He watched her face. Her eyes widened and filled with tears. The shock seemed genuine.

'Dead?'

'Someone murdered him last night. Stabbed him in the back.'

She stared past him, biting the edge of her thumbnail. Tears ran down her face and she made no effort to wipe them away. 'But . . . I don't understand. Where did it happen?'

'In the garage at his home. I found him.' He watched her weep. She had a defeated air. He couldn't feel much sympathy for her when he thought of Georgie Merrell sobbing on the tarmac. 'Cressida, you need to tell me why you were at Lisa's with Harry on the night she died. I don't think you killed her because I cannot believe Harry would have concealed that. Harry's mother is in pieces. Think about that. Think about a woman who has lost her husband and eldest son within months of each other.'

There were footsteps and the sound of running water. She got up and closed a door at the other end of the room, moving sluggishly. She stood at the wide window, looking at the river, laying her head against the glass. When she sat again she pulled her dressing gown tight around her. Her voice was nasal now, as if she had a heavy cold.

'I went to Lisa's flat on my own in a taxi. It was around half five in the morning. Like you said, Lisa was sniffing around my dad again, coming on to him. I knew he had gone to the party. She did his head in, he couldn't say no to her. He had told me she was threatening to close the business as well and I felt bad about that because it was down to my stupidity.' She took a breath, real pain in her voice. 'My mum threw him out in the end because of Lisa. It broke her heart. Everything was destroyed. He has ended up living in a rented place and I can't stand the guy my mum's with now. I flunked out of school at sixteen because everything was messed up. That night Lisa died, I couldn't sleep, thinking about it all. I had met her the week before, you see, and begged her to leave my dad alone. I went to her place and said if she kept the business going, I'd try to get a loan or something to pay towards any compensation awarded to that bloody woman I injured. I told her how sorry I was.' She broke off, panting slightly.

'And Lisa didn't want to know?'

'No. She was on her high horse. Said her life and what she did was none of my affair. She was furious with me for causing the injury and all the hassle it was bringing her way. She told me to get lost or she'd tell my dad . . .' She closed her eyes.

'Tell him you're a sex worker?'

She nodded, wincing.

'How did Lisa know?'

'Harry told her. I don't know why I told him about it and I wish I hadn't. JoJo had warned us all to keep it confidential. He drummed it into us that a high-class operation like this relies on staying hush-hush. I was high on the excitement of it one night. I had earned a lot that week and I was dying to tell someone. I'd met Harry when he visited Body Balm with Lisa. We hit it off straight away. Harry was such a good mate and, well . . . anyway, I talked to him about my work. He got drunk with Lisa one night when she took him to meet that band she sang with and he told her. She was like that. She would weasel things out of people. She didn't know I live here with JoJo. She didn't realise he is involved. Harry wasn't pissed or daft enough to tell her that, he knew it would be dynamite. He was mortified afterwards, asked her not to tell anyone and she said she wouldn't. Oh God, poor Harry! Did he . . . would he have been in much pain?'

'I doubt it. I think he would have died quickly. Let's go back to that night. You took a taxi to Dulwich.'

'I just wanted to try and talk to Lisa again. Plead with her. I couldn't stop thinking about how much trouble she could cause for us. When I got there, the front door had been left open. Her door was open too. I thought there were people still there. Her parties sometimes lasted through to the next morning, especially when they all got wasted. I went in and . . . and she was lying there dead on the sofa. It was horrible, blood all over everything.' She huddled into the chair, gnawing at her thumb again. 'I ran back out into the street. I didn't know what to do. I walked away fast, I just wanted to get away from there. I rang Harry and he came and fetched me from just up the street. You have to believe me, I didn't do it to her. I couldn't stick a knife in anyone!'

No, he couldn't see her doing it. 'There was no one else at the flat?'

'I didn't see anyone. Then that awful thing happened with Harry's dad. We knew he hadn't killed Lisa because he was still at work when I found her. Then Harry reckoned his dad must have seen him when he was coming home and that is why he said he had stabbed her, because he thought Harry was responsible. Oh God, we talked about it for hours, Harry and me, but we couldn't see how we could tell anyone. Harry was out of his mind.'

'You mean you didn't want Harry to tell anyone because your type of sales work would be exposed. You put pressure on him to keep quiet. JoJo Hayworth owns this apartment and runs your business from here, yes?'

She nodded. 'I met him when he was collecting something from Lisa, the time my dad was involved with her. We went for a drink. I came back here with him, slept with him a couple of times. He's a good-looking guy. I was casting around for something to do. He'd had some big wins at the casino, bought this place, was setting up a few girls. He suggested I give this a go, said I could earn well and live in a great apartment.'

'How many of you work for him?'

'Six at the moment. Me and Shelley live here.'

'Running a brothel is a criminal activity, no matter how high class you call it or how upmarket the premises.'

She looked at him with a touch of the old boldness. 'Whatever. It's a good living. I do it because I want to. I have no qualifications and it beats working in a shop. I manage the business on a day-to-day basis, monitor bookings and clientele and JoJo gives me an extra percentage for that. We have more work than we can handle. JoJo is trying to recruit extra staff and set up another flat to work from. I'll manage that one too. I get to live in this lovely place and I make good money. Probably more than you.'

'I expect you do.' He was thinking of a thin, brutalised girl forced to sell sex compared to the lucrative business carried out in this sleek penthouse with customers delivered by chauffeurs. A topsy-turvy world. 'Did JoJo know that Harry had told Lisa about what you do?'

Anxiety crossed her face. 'Not till yesterday. After Lisa died, I thought it didn't matter because we were safe. But he was here when Harry rang me yesterday and said he couldn't keep quiet any longer. JoJo heard bits of the conversation and he could see how stressed out I was, so in the end I had to tell him. He was furious with me for telling Harry about our set-up here. I wish . . . I wish I never had. But he knew Harry had agreed not to tell you.'

'Where is JoJo now?'

'I don't know. I haven't seen him since yesterday. I think he had a shoot.'

'He didn't come back last night?'

'No. he's got a girlfriend somewhere, he often stays at hers.' The penny slowly dropped and she sat forward. 'Oh no! You don't think JoJo had anything to do with Harry . . . ?'

'Your guess is as good as mine. JoJo has a lot to lose here if word gets out. I'm not sure that prosecution for keeping a brothel would fit with his modelling image or impress his employers. He could go to prison. He would lose all his sources of income as well as having a criminal record. You don't know where this girlfriend lives?'

'No idea.'

'Was JoJo in London the night Lisa was killed?'

'I . . . I don't think so . . . No, no, he wasn't, he was away working, abroad, I think. Hang on.' She reached for her phone and scrolled through. 'Yes, he was in Ibiza.'

He turned and looked out of the window to watch the river running. He heard Cressida sniffing and blowing her nose. He stood and looked at her. She seemed to be shedding years and sophistication by the minute. Now she looked about twelve. The damaged, angry girl inside the glamorous shell was all too visible.

'Harry went through a lot for you. He ended up torn apart by wanting to keep his promise to you, because he had given away your secret, and through grief for his father and his family. He was in bits, at war with himself. You kept him in an impossible position, you know that?'

'I didn't know what else to do. We couldn't think of any way to keep this set-up out of it if we told the police what had happened. We knew it would come out.' She started crying in earnest, talking through sobs. 'We were good friends, me and Harry, really close. We talked about everything. We were both mad at our dads, we'd both had our families ripped apart. We *got* each other. We talked about Lisa. He liked her. She was funny, good company, she talked to him about his drumming, treated him like a little brother and he enjoyed that. But then he hated himself for it because she had replaced his mother. There was nothing else between them. I can see why you might think that but there wasn't. He was such a good bloke. He didn't judge me for being an escort. I can't believe this. It's too horrible!'

'You need to tell the truth now. Harry's father suffered in ways that you don't even know about. Harry's mother and brother are suffering right this minute. You have to call the police. I'll be contacting them about you anyway, and about JoJo.' He wrote down Kharal's number and passed it to her.

She raised her puffy face. 'What will my dad say?'

'He loves you. He'll stand by you. I'm going now. Make that call to the police.' He moved away and stopped. 'I'm about to have a daughter. I wouldn't want her to end up selling sex, no matter how glamorous the address or how much she earned from it. Wash your face and pick up the phone.'

She got up slowly. 'What if JoJo comes back?'

'The police will deal with him. I don't think he will be back here for now, but don't say anything to him about this if he does turn up in the meantime. In fact, bolt the door and call the police if he comes back and tries to get in. He could turn violent.'

He drove to a nearby garage, bought a coffee and sat in the car sipping it. He didn't want to talk to Kharal. He emailed him, telling him that Cressida Wellings would be ringing the police and why and giving him JoJo Hayworth's address in Canterbury. Hayworth must be the likely suspect for Harry's murder but if he had been abroad when Lisa was killed, then the perpetrator was still to be found. He pictured Merrell lying, despairing and hopeless on the bed in that awful hotel basement that was so much like a prison cell.

Suddenly, he longed to see Ruth. He was supposed to make a statement but it could wait until later. He rang her, holding his breath for that moment when he would hear her say his name.

* * *

He had driven on to Brighton and was sitting with Ruth in a sun-filled conservatory full of plants and books. Emlyn Williams was attending various therapy sessions at a private clinic and would be out until late afternoon. They were sharing a lunch of cheese, fruit and pasta salad from a tray. Swift had sat outside the handsome, detached house for some time when he arrived, wanting to ring the bell and needing to drive away again, fast. The house and its occupants were too real — wisteria arching over the porch, window boxes of violas, a pale pink magnolia surrounded by bluebells. Finally, Ruth had opened the door and stood there, looking at him, holding out a hand.

'Does Emlyn know I'm here?' he asked.

'Yes, I rang him. No secrets. He was fine. There's no anger left in him, Ty. He's burnt out and just grateful that I came back. Too grateful, almost. He keeps thanking me and it makes me uncomfortable.'

On the way in, he had glanced into the downstairs room that had obviously been adapted for Williams — a high hospital bed with levers and a table across it, a hoist, and a chair with footrests. The diminished, cramped life of an invalid.

'I'm glad you came here,' she continued. 'I know it was hard for you. A pain barrier.'

'Yes. Well, I am here. And you're really okay?'

'Honestly, nothing to worry about. Just my bones and ligaments limbering up for the big push.'

'Are you frightened? I am!'

She laughed and nudged him. 'Not frightened, a bit apprehensive. Who wouldn't be? It's good to be home, good to have you here. Tell me about you. Your poor nose!'

He brought her up to date about the investigation and about Yana.

'I don't think she'll agree to be a witness, she's too scared. When I've wrapped up this case, I want to try to help her move somewhere. I've had an idea I'll work on.'

'Do you think you are close to resolving the Merrell case?'

'I feel as if I'm wearing a blindfold. It's just there, within reach, but I can't locate it.' He took her hand. 'That young woman I saw this morning, Cressida. She's so angry with her parents. I wonder what Branna will make of us and our confusion?'

She put his hand against her stomach. 'We can only love her and do our best.'

He said nothing but thought, *yes, but will that be enough?* He pictured a future with visits to see Branna timed around a sick man's medical appointments. Instead of an illicit lover, he would be an illicit father.

'Do you want to see her room?' Ruth asked.

They went upstairs to a room overlooking the garden. It smelled of fresh paint. The walls were a pale primrose. There was a crib ready, with a tiny white duvet and a mobile of brightly coloured animals suspended over it. A plastic table with a changing mat stood prepared, with packs of nappies on a shelf beneath.

'I should buy her things. What should I buy?'

Ruth set the mobile spinning. 'Clothes, toys, whatever takes your fancy. Indulge yourself. Listen, the mobile can play tunes.'

She pressed a button and a lullaby started. She moved to him and put her head against his chest. He circled her with his arms, inhaling the warm scent of her hair. For a moment, it all made sense.

* * *

Kharal caught up with him after he had made his statement, bristling up to him in the corridor of the police station.

'How come you didn't mention Cressida Wellings and JoJo Hayworth when we spoke before?'

'I didn't put to and two together until I got home and thought about it. It's been a complicated enquiry and it was all a bit traumatic. You know, finding Harry Merrell like that.'

Kharal looked unconvinced. 'You shouldn't have gone to see Wellings. I could have you for tampering with witnesses.' There was a suppressed energy to the man, a contained aggression.

'I suppose. Still, you got a good lead from her so it worked in your favour. Have you found Hayworth?'

'Not yet, we will. Stay away from witnesses, Swift, or I'll have you. I don't care who you're related to. The Queen could be your aunty but I'll have you.'

'They're all yours,' he said mildly.

'Anything else you're not telling me?'

'No. I'm still looking for Lisa Eastwood's killer. I'll keep you posted.'

Kharal glared, spun on his heel and walked away, clicking his fingers at a minion.

Mary had texted him, saying that Simone was on a training course in Birmingham and would he like to meet up? They decided to eat in the Silver Mermaid. Swift hailed a cab and checked his emails on the way there. There was one from Cressida:

I've talked to the police. My dad is here now. I'm going to stay with him until I sort something out. I've been going over and over everything and I thought I should tell you something I remembered. When I went to see Lisa the week before she died, there was a guy there with her. She told him to go and wait in the kitchen while we talked. I didn't know him. A tall guy, about your height, blondish hair, fit looking. He had an expensive watch. That's all. C

A stillness came over him. He saw the pieces finally coming together, the picture making sense. It added up, of course, that Lisa would have pursued every man who came into her orbit, not caring what territory she was trespassing in or the hurt she might cause. It was just how she operated, a compulsion, almost. Richard Molina had said that she was like a kid in a sweetie shop where men were concerned, liking to pick and mix. He decided that there was no need to rush. For tonight, he would slow things down, enjoy his meal with Mary and give his aching bones a rest.

She was waiting when he arrived, working on her laptop. They both ordered red wine and lasagne.

'To our pregnant women,' Mary said, raising her glass and running a hand through her springy hair. 'I don't want to sound disloyal but it is a relief to have a day without reports of baby's movements. I get a text or email pretty much hourly, but Simone's had to turn her phone off today.'

Swift drank deeply. It was wonderful to see her alone. Restful. But he wouldn't say so. 'Have you got a name yet?'

'We can't decide. We like Alric — that was Simone's dad's name, and Donal. I said we should wait for the baby and see which name suits him.'

'I saw Ruth today. We're going to call the baby Branna.'

'Ah, good,' Mary said softly. 'How did that go, seeing her?'

'Surprisingly okay. I went to Brighton, to her house. Her husband was out at physio.'

Mary was always one for cutting to the chase. 'Do you think you two will get together when he dies?'

'I've no idea. Who knows what we'll feel?'

'Hmm, best to just play it day by day.'

He changed the subject, not wanting to dwell on it now. 'Just in case you get any feedback, I've had a run in with a DCI Laith Kharal over a murder in Balham. We share a mutual antipathy. He thinks I want special treatment because we're related.'

'Okay. If he crosses my radar, I'll let you know. Oh look! Here's double trouble.'

Cedric was coming in with his friend Milo. They both liked vibrant colours and egged each other on in their wardrobe choices. Tonight, Cedric was wearing a violet shirt with pink checks and Milo sported a cerise T-shirt patterned with raspberries. These days he walked slowly, bowed forward, with two sticks so that he resembled a flamboyant tortoise as he edged into his seat.

'We're just thinking about pudding,' Swift told them.

'Have the lemon meringue,' Milo said. 'I'll share yours if you get two spoons. Must make sure you keep your gorgeous physique.'

Milo always flirted with him and regularly expressed his disappointment that Swift was straight and not open to offers.

'How's Yana?' Swift asked.

Cedric nodded. 'She's okay. Becoming a little edgy from not getting out, but keeping herself busy with cooking and practising her flute now her chest has cleared up. I'm eating well and listening to beautiful music. She's relieved that her tests came back clear so she has no other health problems.'

'And being a witness?'

Cedric shook his head. 'She hasn't changed her mind.'

Cedric explained Yana's story to Mary while Milo ate most of Swift's pudding. They played dominoes until late. Swift was so tired he almost nodded off in his chair. Mary hopped into a taxi while Cedric and Milo walked him home between them, saying that the young had no stamina these days.

CHAPTER 13

The sun woke Swift the following morning, strong and bright, working its way through a chink in the curtains and spilling a lemony light across his face. He did some stretches and took deep breaths, reckoning he should manage to get on the river in a couple of days. His nose now looked as if he'd had a bad cold rather than a punch. He ate toast, crunching it as he walked outside with his coffee and sat on the swing seat, deep in thought. He spent the hour between eight and nine cleaning, loading the washing machine and putting accumulated newspapers in the recycling bin. At the stroke of nine, he rang Tracey and Siddons, Estate Agents, and asked for Louise Pullman.

'How can I help you this morning?' she asked cheerily.

'Hi, Louise, it's Tyrone Swift here, the private investigator. We met at Finbar's a while ago and you gave me your card.'

'Oh, yes. Are you in the market?'

'A friend might be, fairly soon. Could you tell me what percentage you charge?'

He listened while she rattled on about ballpark figures and market values.

'Okay, thanks. That's really helpful. By the way, you know you had flu when Lisa Eastwood had her party. Were you at Finbar's that night? I expect he looked after you.'

'The party? Oh, that's right, I had a high temperature. No, I stayed at mine that weekend. I felt rotten and I didn't want to pass it on. Fin's a bit of a hypochondriac when it comes to germs.'

She didn't ask him why he wanted to know.

'I'm the same with bugs, I'm afraid. Probably a man thing.'

She giggled. 'I know, you're all wimps really! Fin ended up catching some kind of flu anyway. He has had a virus for weeks now, it has really worn him down. I kept nagging him to take a break and finally he has. He has gone away for a few days. Well, and of course he was ever so upset at what he found out about Dominic, the adoption and everything. All that awful stuff about his real parents. It really knocked the stuffing out of Fin. I've never seen him look so gutted. He hasn't been right since, so the break should do him good.'

'Has he gone somewhere nice?'

'Nice enough. He's at his place in Dorset, a little holiday cottage he bought a couple of years ago.'

'Lovely.'

'Well, he needed to go there anyway because something went wrong with the boiler, so he had to sort it out. He should be back in a couple of days but the plumber is being unreliable. It's hard to talk to him because the mobile signal is useless there.'

'Great, though, having a place in the country. Is it out in the sticks?'

'Sort of. It's near a little village called Hinbury Magna.'

'Well, anyway, thanks so much for your advice and I'll tell my friend.'

He put the phone down, recalling Power's ashen face when he had learned of Merrell's adoption, how his voice had hoarsened when Swift mentioned the abortion. The man was ill but it wasn't flu. It was a different, deeper malaise. He had called Lisa an angel and a devil. Swift now knew why, and why he was hiding with his torment, just as his friend had hidden in the bowels of the Hays hotel.

He turned immediately to google and found Hinbury Magna, situated between Dorchester and Lyme Regis, a couple of miles inland from the coast. A quick route check told him he could drive it in about three and a half hours. He confirmed with Cedric that it was okay to borrow the car again and was on the road within the hour.

* * *

The M3 was fast until just past Winchester, where there had been an accident. It was warm, the sky a translucent blue. Swift took off his jacket and rolled up his shirtsleeves. As the queue of cars inched forwards, he listened to one of Cedric's tapes of Cajun music. The bottleneck eased after ten miles and he reached the A35 at Dorchester by noon. Five miles on, he turned on to a B road with a signpost to Hinbury Magna and Hinbury Parva. The road curved down into a valley, over a humpback bridge, then right to Hinbury Magna, which was circled by soft green hills. The verges were covered with pale yellow and cream primroses and violets. A stream ran to the left and through the village, dividing it in two, with cottages built of stone and flint clustered on either side of it.

Swift pulled in near a village smithy beside a chestnut tree, advertising working weekends and holiday tuition in blacksmithing skills, hedging and dry-stone walling. He got out of the car and stretched. All was quiet. To his right was a post office with mullioned windows, a vicarage and a village hall with a large sign indicating that a WI market was in progress with teas, coffees and light lunches available. A good prospect for information as well as food.

He walked to the single-storey, brick-built hall. The loud buzz of conversation within was astonishing after the silence outside. Delicious smells greeted him as he let the swing doors close behind him. He identified coffee, vanilla, chocolate and lemon. The wooden floor was faded from use and the walls were painted a dull green that reminded him of hospitals. Stalls lined both sides of the deep room, piled with cakes of all shapes and sizes, biscuits, pies, filled rolls, jams, chutneys and preserves. There was also a table with children's clothes and toys. The place was thronged, mainly with women, most of them young. He could see two men, the vicar, with black shirt and dog collar, and a man about Cedric's age. A woman in her thirties, wearing jeans and a polo-neck jumper approached him, smiling, licking her fingers.

'Can we help you?'

'I'd love a sandwich and a coffee.'

'Come this way, I'm in charge of the lunches today.'

She led him to the lunch stall where he bought a ham and tomato roll and a large mug of coffee, all for under two pounds.

'I've never mingled with the WI before. I expected it would be grey-haired ladies of a certain age, all swapping recipes.' His stepmother, Joyce, was a member in London. She was in her sixties, bustling, an organiser by nature, a bit of a do-gooder.

'You need to check your stereotypes. Our group is fairly new. I started it with a friend a couple of years ago. I had moved here from Southampton and needed some company. We had thirty members within a couple of months, lots of women who've given up work temporarily to look after children, who needed a social network.'

'You do swap recipes, though? I'd find it reassuring.'

She laughed. 'I will concede that we occasionally do that. You don't look as if that's what you're here for though.'

'I'm trying to find an old friend. Maybe you can help me. His name is Finbar Power. He lives in London but has a holiday place somewhere nearby.'

'Not sure, but I think I've heard the name. Hang on.'

She turned to a woman at the next stall who was selling potted plants, and waited for her to complete a purchase. Swift finished his roll and drank the coffee, which was fresh and robust. He looked around at the brisk trading at the stalls. Several of them had almost emptied since he walked in and tidying and sweeping had begun. The vicar was making his way through a huge slice of Victoria sponge, balancing his plate as he spoke to a sturdy woman in tweeds and mucky wellingtons. Everyone looked well fed and affluent. All the faces were white. He was aware of the parallel lives being led in this one country, never touching each other. He felt as if he had crossed an invisible border somewhere between London and this rural haven.

The friendly woman came back to him. 'Thought Tilda would know, she knows everyone. He's at Hasilbeare Cottage. It's about ten minutes' drive out of the village towards Hinbury Parva. She says you can't miss it, it's set back from the road with a grey front door and the name's on the gate. Tilda says he's about, she saw him in the post office and her nephew services the boiler.'

He thanked her and wandered around the stalls. He bought tomato and fig preserves and a fruitcake. He stopped at the children's stall, choosing a perky-looking knitted giraffe and a tiny damson-coloured patchwork jacket. It felt odd, handing over the money, knowing that they were for his daughter.

* * *

The road towards Hinbury Parva curved nearer to the coast. After a mile or two Swift could smell the sea, then he caught the odd glimpse of silvery blue shimmering across the fields. The breeze had strengthened from the west and scraps of thin white cloud drifted across the sky. He knew that the meeting that was to come would expose layers of pain and he drove slowly, postponing it.

He found the cottage easily and parked across the road, where there was a grassy layby. It was double fronted, compact and built of honey-coloured stone with a Virginia creeper covering the front and bordering the bow windows. A small front garden lay behind a low stone wall. It was well tended, with lavender, geraniums, poppies and candytuft growing in profusion. There was a scent of woodsmoke in the air, sweet and pungent. The silence was profound. No answer came to his knock. He shaded his eyes and looked through a front window into an empty sitting room with a deep fireplace stacked with logs, easy chairs and a table covered with paperbacks.

A flagstone path ran around the side of the cottage. Swift followed it to a lush back garden filled with shrubs, roses and a large bank of thyme and camomile. Finbar Power was midway down, cutting back dark green ivy and throwing the branches into a wheelbarrow. When Swift called his name he turned and stared. Then his lips moved and he nodded, as if confirming something to himself.

Swift stood still and waited while he drew off his gardening gloves, threw them on top of the pile of ivy in the barrow and walked slowly over to him. Power was pale, despite the sunny day.

'How did you find me?'

'Louise.'

'I see.' His jeans were flecked with mud, his walking boots caked in soil and bits of leaves. 'I've been tidying. It has been warm and damp here for a while. Everything starts growing like crazy. Nature's mad dash to summer.'

'I can see it would take a lot of maintenance. It's a lovely spot.'

'Yes. The cottage is seventeenth century. Very olde England for an Irishman. It was used in a film some time back, before I bought it. One of the Thomas Hardy novels, I can't remember which one. One of those tales of betrayal and sadness and tragedy set in pastoral beauty.'

'Louise said you haven't been well.'

His eyes were steady but held a far-off look. 'She fusses too much. I had a bad time with that virus, that's all. A bit of sea fishing has helped.'

'All? She said what you'd found out about Dominic upset you terribly.'

He looked down. 'It did, yes.'

'But it's not just what you found out, is it? It's far more than that, a series of terrible events. That's why you are here, hiding away.'

Power raised his eyes. They were dimmed now, full of hurt. 'Yes, it's all much more. Much too much.'

Swift could see that there would be no bluffing and he was relieved. He kept his voice low and steady.

'I don't believe in a virus, unless you call guilt and remorse a virus. I can see why you wanted to come here, it's a place that could help with healing. But I don't think it is helping you. You don't look as if you have benefited. How could you? I know what happened. Not all the details but the general outline.'

Power rubbed a finger. 'I got a splinter in here yesterday and I just can't dig it out. Amazing how a small sliver of rose bush can be so annoying. I put some of this ointment on that's supposed to draw it out but I don't think it works.' He blinked rapidly. 'I was horrified and relieved when you told me Georgie wanted you to investigate. When I've been lying awake in the dark, which has been every night, I thought that you would work it out somehow. You read people and you seem tenacious. I think I wanted you to find out, lift the burden from me. I told you about the loan to Dominic to keep you interested in me. I suppose I wanted to be seen as someone who had done some good, shown some kindness as well.'

They stood for a moment under the shifting clouds, the light spilling onto their faces as the sun moved around towards the western sky.

'Will you tell me now?' Swift asked.

Power took a breath. 'Let's walk. It will be easier if we're walking. This way.'

A wooden gate at the end of the garden led to a stile with access to a path across fields. They kept to the left hand boundary, walking along a rough, stony track. The wind stirred the grasses and rustled in the thick hedges. They were the only people in the landscape.

'I've got to know a fair bit about the area,' Power said quietly. 'I saw a Peregrine falcon last time I was down here. You probably know that the place is littered with fossils.'

'I came to Lyme Regis once with my parents. We went fossil hunting. I was very excited when I found an ichthyosaur vertebra and a calcified ammonite.'

Power's voice cracked suddenly. 'She told me the baby was mine. She said she was going to have it. She started by saying she wanted me to leave Louise. She threatened that she would tell her about us and the pregnancy if I didn't. I didn't know she'd had an abortion.'

'When did it start, your relationship with Lisa?'

'About eight months ago. She had always flirted with me but I never took much notice. It was just the way she was with any man she met. I found her attractive, of course. What man wouldn't? But Dom was my friend — and I love Louise. It took me a long time to find her and we plan to marry next year, start a family. Oh, I don't know why I got involved with Lisa, it just happened. She came into the shop one day, saying she wanted to set up an aquarium. It was just an excuse. I think she was attracted to my wealth rather than me. She knew I had made a fortune in the markets, Dom had told her. She looked so beautiful and . . . anyway, I have no defence to make. I knew deep down that it would cause trouble but she was reckless and I found it contagious. I was giddy, like a teenager again. She was so much fun. After a couple of months, I couldn't deal with the deception, the furtiveness. I told her I wanted to end it. I was riddled with guilt about Dom. That's when she announced the pregnancy. You know, I think she wanted to get rid of Dom and it was her way of doing it. She had seen photos of the cottage and asked me about it. She went on and on about how the two of us could come and live here, get away from everything in London, start a new life. She thought she had it all worked out, this other existence. It was utterly ridiculous, even if I had been tempted. Lisa wouldn't have lasted five minutes in the countryside. She was an urban creature. She was furious when I told her that and refused to bring her here. She was so used to getting what she wanted, throwing people away when she'd had enough of them. When I told her I didn't want to leave Louise and I didn't want a child with her, she turned nasty.' He stopped on the track, his hands bunched in his pockets. 'But she'd got rid of the baby anyway.'

'Yes. I don't believe Lisa intended to have another child. It was a bargaining tool.'

They walked on, through a small coppice of ash trees and over another stile into an undulating meadow. A herd of cows were grazing in the distance, several fields over.

'She was broke, you know, almost as broke as Dom,' Power said. 'There was some big problem with her business and she always spent like there was no tomorrow. I went to see her when he was at work, tried to persuade her to break things off. She said if I gave her twenty thousand, she would get rid of the baby and agree to say nothing more. I didn't trust her. I thought she was lying. Lisa was greedy, greedy for affection, money, people, and things. There was an air of desperation about her, too. She was running out of options and it was making her act wildly. I'm wealthy but I could see a future of more demands for cash, and it all constantly hanging over me.' He laughed. 'Ironic really, I'd already given Dom money and she was after more. I can see now that she played me. I think a pay-off was always her goal but I didn't realise that at the time.'

'Did you go to her flat the night of the party, in the early hours?'

His voice brimmed with emotion. 'I hated her by then. I was obsessed by feelings of hatred, day and night. I felt so bad about Dom, about betraying him. She was set to ruin everything in my life, my friendship, my relationship. Louise is so kind and caring towards me, always looking out for me. Lisa had already caused Dom's family awful suffering. I knew that she would tire of Dom and me and eventually move on to some other man and leave my life broken. That is what she did, it was how she lived. I don't believe she ever thought about the hurt she caused. It just didn't impinge on her. She thought she had a right to take whatever she wanted. That sounds as if I am trying to justify violence. I'm not and I know it sounds pathetic. In the end I was no better than she was, I deceived and lied. I brooded about it all. I cursed myself for having got involved with her. I persuaded myself that I would be doing Dom, me and so many other people a favour by getting rid of her. I even told myself that it might mean Dom would go to back to Georgie and his sons so it would be a bad means to a good end.' He paused and rubbed at his forehead. It was glistening with sweat. 'I got to her place about four a.m. I waited in the hall downstairs until there was no more noise. There's a little recess under the stairwell. I knew they kept a key under the doormat but the door had been left open. I used one of my fishing knives. It was quick, simple. She was lying on the sofa, dead drunk and I could almost persuade myself I had just extended her sleep. She gave one groan, that was all. I felt such tremendous relief.' He stopped again, gazed at Swift. He looked like a man who has been told he has a terminal illness. 'I'm not a bad person. At least, I wasn't. I know what I am now. Unspeakable.'

They had reached a fallen tree trunk, a thick birch covered in moss and lichen. Power sank onto it and Swift sat also, sensing the man's desperation.

'At least you acknowledge that,' he said.

Power shuddered. 'Don't try to be kind. I don't deserve it. I know I'm a monster. I feel like a reservoir of poison amidst all this beauty. I thought Lisa was still pregnant. I was prepared to kill an unborn child as well as its mother. I have left her other young child motherless. I have hardly slept since. I fled down here to try to work up the courage to hand myself in. I couldn't look at Louise. I've been using the story of a virus to avoid her. I could hardly speak to Georgie and I should have been offering her comfort and support, helping her with the boys. I tortured my best friend, a man who had only ever shown me kindness and understanding. He had been through terrible turmoil, finding out about his parents and he killed himself for something I had done. And in the end, there wasn't even a baby. Louise might have forgiven me for having an affair but a child . . . Dom would never have forgiven me and why should he have? A family left without a father. Oh God. How did this happen?'

Swift gazed at the horizon. He could hear the sea, restless and booming, see foam flecks. They were high up here, they must be near the cliffs. There was more to be told, more that would add to Power's grief but he would have to know and perhaps it would also relieve him of some guilt.

'Finbar, Dominic didn't kill himself just because of Lisa and his emotions about his parents. Something else happened that night, something connected to another man Lisa had been involved with. It meant that Harry Merrell was near Lisa's flat on his scooter, helping a friend. Dominic saw him. He thought his son had murdered Lisa. I think that was his main motive for taking the blame and killing himself. He was in a state of great confusion and emotion. He felt overwhelming guilt for the course his life had taken. I believe he saw everything as a dreadful re-enactment of his father stabbing his mother.'

Power said nothing. His gaunt profile lifted to the sky, his mouth hung open. Swift decided to say nothing for now about Harry's death. The man could only absorb so much and he would find out soon enough. The baby might not even have been Power's, he thought. Perry Wellings might have been the father. Lisa might not have been sure herself. Rooks were cawing and squabbling in a tall oak nearby, then flew away, taking their racket with them.

'That song, *When a Man Loves a Woman,*' Power said after a while, 'It was so true for Dominic. He could have written it. He was a good man who made the one huge mistake. All this, all this damage and hurt. Yet the sun keeps shining, the world spinning, and the tide rushing in and out.' He pressed his hands hard against the rough bark beneath him. 'Courage. It has to come down to courage. I have been trying to find it and failing until now. I'm glad you came, you've given me the spur I needed.'

He gave Swift a sad, hopeless look, then sprang up and started running fast towards the horizon, yelling loudly, one long, savage note. *No, not that,* Swift thought and ran after him, not wasting his breath with shouting. His ribs protested as he raced. There was just grass now, slightly slippery from the sea spray. The breeze blew salt into his eyes as the ground tilted over a slight ridge and then downwards. The cliff edge was suddenly there in the distance, and the surging waves below. Power was at the edge. He stopped for a moment, looked up to the sky, then put out his arms as if preparing to dive, threw himself forward and vanished.

Swift reached the edge and looked over. It was more than forty metres down to the base. Power lay face down on a small strip of scree and jagged rock. His head looked broken, his right leg bent and misshapen, both arms twisted. It was a fairly calm day, but the sea was powerful and massive looking. The pounding waves were near to Power's head but as he watched, Swift judged that the tide was retreating. He rang emergency services, cursing the poor phone signal and huddling away from the snapping breeze. He described the location as clearly as he could, straining to hear and be heard. He had to repeat himself several times, shouting over the noisy tumult of the surf below.

He looked at the shoreline. The strip of shingle ended on each side in an outcrop of huge boulders and pools, where the sea crashed and swirled. As the tide ebbed, it exposed glittering shards of rock. Along the cliff and its fringe of swaying grasses, he saw a small break about twenty metres to his right, with a narrow shale track winding down. It was steep with deep cracks and crevices. He knew that the cliffs in this area were unstable and prone to landslides. He knew too that Power was unlikely to have survived such a plunge but he had to check. He ran along and eased over the edge, crouching as he started to scrabble and slide down the rough, spiky limestone, catching at tufts of grass to balance. Half way down, his hand slipped and he braced himself against the friable shale underfoot, trying to dig his heels in but sliding uncontrollably. He travelled several metres, panic seizing him, desperately trying to find a foothold as dust and stones flew. His jeans ripped and he felt a stab of pain in his left calf as his skin tore. At last, he managed to grab a thin spear of rock. His face was damp with sweat and spray, his mouth dry. He tensed his leg muscles and continued down.

Seagulls screamed and swooped overhead, mocking his clumsy descent. His hands were shredded and bleeding and his chest aching as he reached the bottom, falling on to the rocks. Sweat now covered his face and trickled into his eyes. Panting, he righted himself and walked to Power's body. He saw that the head was smashed and badly lacerated, with bone and brain matter visible through a huge gash in the skull.

He walked to the sea, dipped his hands in the water and threw some on his face. The salt nipped and stung his ripped skin but he was glad of it, exhilarated almost. He sat exhausted on the hard, damp scree. His leg was bleeding from a long graze and he wiped the blood away with a flap of denim from his jeans. For a moment on the cliff, he had thought he might die, that two bodies would be found. He closed his eyes and listened to the relentless sea music, glad to be breathing. He had dreamed about falling from a cliff, particularly after Ruth had left him. Terrifying dreams, tipping into the void and waking just before hitting the ground. He had read that such dreams symbolised feelings of loss of control or fear of failure. No such frights and nightmares for Power now.

His phone rang, breaking his reverie. He was told that an air ambulance was ten minutes away. He explained that he had descended to the body and was instructed to stay where he was. He stayed by Power, watching the sea. The sky had clouded and the breeze was growing chiller in the late afternoon. He pulled his jacket close to his body, shivering slightly with tiredness and shock. Then he heard the approaching growl of the helicopter as it rattled from the left, traversing the sky. It was bright yellow, twin engine and as it came nearer and lower, the noise was deafening.

Swift stood, watching as someone was winched down to the shore. It was a woman, in green overalls. She unclipped herself, glanced at the body and came over to Swift.

'You okay?'

'Yes. I saw what happened. His name's Finbar Power and he's dead.'

'Righto. I'm Marie. I need to take a look and call for a stretcher. Can you sit out of the way for now? We'll winch you up soon.'

He backed away and sat on a rock, watching as another paramedic was lowered, then a stretcher. They manoeuvred Power's body on and strapped him down, signalling for him to be winched up. The tremendous noise of the engines vibrated through Swift and he felt suddenly nauseous and put his head down, concentrating on breaths. They winched him up next, then the two crew members, and the helicopter veered and climbed.

Marie put a red blanket around him, looked at his hands and leg and took his pulse. She cleaned his skin with antiseptic wipes, telling him he needed to be checked over in hospital. He sat back and watched the sea glide below, the colour lightening as land approached and the helicopter's shadow danced like a huge dragonfly over the fields.

* * *

Georgie Merrell was wearing a plaster on her left arm. It was a bright, jolly blue. She had tripped over Sid on the stairs.

'So clumsy of me,' she said.

'Grief makes us clumsy. Forgetful, too.' Swift had insisted on making coffee and put the cup in front of her.

They sat in her kitchen. Adam was at school. Sid lay in his basket sleeping and snuffling. Georgie looked as if she was fading away, yet she had regained the composure Swift had witnessed at their first meeting.

'At least it's my left arm. I can draw and paint, carry on working. Keep myself sort of sane.'

'It helps.'

'Look at your poor hands, all scratched.'

He had a few plasters over the worst tears and a bandage on his leg. 'I'll mend. The helicopter ride was the worst bit. It was the first time I'd been in one and I wouldn't want to repeat the experience.'

They had talked it all through, all the details. She needed to go over and over it.

'No wonder Finbar didn't come near us. It hurt, you know, that he stayed away, even after Dominic died. At the funeral he was remote, hardly said a word. I asked him if he would do a reading but he said he wasn't up to it. I thought it was shock. I was fond of him and I knew how much he meant to Dominic. At our wedding, when he was best man, he said we were the perfect match, like a pair of bookends.' She sipped her coffee, added several spoons of sugar. 'If Lisa hadn't contacted me, none of this would ever have happened. One animal portrait caused four deaths. I keep thinking it's all my fault.'

'You know that's not true. You're thinking that way because you are so tired and sad. Lisa was a catalyst. Finbar Power called her an angel and a devil. I know what he meant. She was a complex woman. She took a lot of risks and in the end, she ran out of luck. She had tired of your husband. She was in dire straits financially and Dominic couldn't come up with any more money. Money drove her, as well as the need for admiration and a desire to get her own way. A lot of things weren't working out for her. Her business was being sued and she must have known that would go badly. She had tried to get funds out of her husband but he wouldn't play ball. Her father had told her he wasn't in a position to sub her further. I think she was getting desperate for money by the time Finbar stabbed her.'

'Poor Dominic. So much anguish. I wish he had come and talked to me. I would have taken him back. The debts, the secrecy about the adoption . . . none of that would have mattered.'

'I think it was too late for him. He had gone to a very dark place. His mind was full of images of blood and death and he had been brooding on them for a while. He had been treading water for a long time and getting into difficulties with money. He must have known that Lisa's interest in him was on the wane. Dominic was an intelligent man and he would have realised that he couldn't hang on to her. He had thrown away his marriage, his compass in life. If he had found out the truth about the circumstances of his adoption when he was with you, he would have coped. But then, I think it was the rupture caused by leaving you that prompted him to seek information about his birth parents. People go searching when life is uncertain. You once said he was your north star but you see, I think you were his too. The way things came together for him was overwhelming. He sat in the basement of the Hays hotel and the events of his life merged in a terrible maelstrom.'

'A kind of breakdown.'

'Yes, devastating.'

'That woman. She exerted so much of a hold. She played with Harry, too. Didn't she have any conscience?'

'I don't believe there was any relationship other than friendship between her and Harry, if that's of any comfort. I think she was a prima donna and that egotism overruled any moral qualms. She was certainly part of a strange, volatile network. Of course, no one forced those men to get involved. It was their choice. Hayworth took her money, two of the others said they would leave their wives for her and didn't. One took her life. They caused their own anguish for themselves and their families. She was used as well.'

JoJo Hayworth had been found at his girlfriend's flat and was in police custody. He had confessed to the stabbing of Harry Merrell in an effort to protect his prostitution business. He had just bought another flat in Putney to extend his enterprise. There had been too much at stake to risk Harry's promise of staying quiet. One of Kharal's minions had phoned Swift to tell him. There had been no acknowledgement or hint of appreciation for his help.

Swift asked how Adam was coping.

'I'm not sure. He seems okay. Tearful at times and Sid is getting a lot of cuddles. He has a lovely teacher at school and she is being very kind. It's hard to know what to tell him. I don't want to upset him too much. There is a police liaison person who is good, too. He's calling again tomorrow.'

They sat and Swift listened to Georgie repeating her questions and comments. He gave her the same answers as the clock ticked on. She seemed to find some comfort in the constant reassurance. He made more coffee while she talked about meeting Dominic, their life together and the holidays they had enjoyed, the way he had been with the boys. She recalled all kinds of anecdotes, mining deep into her layers of memory. He remembered Harry's jibe, asking if he was a shrink. As he listened to Georgie's monologue, he felt like an unskilled therapist. He supposed that just being there and listening was of some small help.

The sun highlighted greasy patches on the windows. The rubbish bin needed emptying, the cookbook still lay open at the same recipe he had seen on his last visit and the house looked forlorn and dusty. He thought it would take Georgie a long time to emerge from the stupor of shock and misery.

CHAPTER 14

Nora had phoned him to report that the brothel in Bolton had been located and raided and one of the owners arrested. Her colleagues there believed that the second man involved in running it had fled abroad. As soon as he heard the news, Swift had gone to see Malory Meredith, taking two boxes of Striped Tiger cheroots. This time, he gave her a hug when he arrived. They had sat in her cluttered living room and talked through what had happened to Lisa and the reasons. Swift was careful about the details he shared and about apportioning blame. He wasn't in the business of hurting her any more than he had to, or tarnishing her memories of her friend. She was astute enough to make her own deductions as she puffed on a cheroot.

'What will happen to Tamsin?' she asked. 'That poor child. Like Dominic, she has lost both parents. I presume her father might be in prison for a long time.'

'I'd say so. I spoke to Donald Eastwood. He is going to come back and see her and her grandmother. He seems keen on the idea of taking Tamsin back home with him to Cape Town. Talked about having a huge house and gardens and a pool, getting a nanny. I suppose he sees it as a second chance at raising a child. Of course, JoJo Hayworth would have to agree to it but he might see it as the best option. I wouldn't be surprised if Mrs Hayworth is keen on it, especially if Mr Eastwood offers a sweetener as part of the arrangement.' He entertained gloomy thoughts about Eastwood's indulgent parenting producing another self-obsessed young woman but chided himself that he had better see how he turned out as a father before casting aspersions.

'Money,' Malory said. 'It causes trouble and eases trouble.'

He had watched again as her hands trembled with the coffee cups. Then he had told her the story of a girl from Syria and put a proposal to her. After some detailed discussion, she had agreed and he said he would speak to Yana about the idea.

Three days later, at the beginning of May, Swift drove Cedric and Yana to Dulwich with her small bag of possessions. She was wearing new jeans and shirt and looked like any other teenager, her hair twisted in a knot. Malory had made up carefully for her visitors and was wearing a red silk trouser suit with a red and white scarf at her neck. Bertram was in her arms when she opened the door and Yana immediately took him and cuddled him.

Swift made coffee and cleared spaces on chairs. Malory had clearly been attempting to tidy up but this had resulted in more haphazard, tilting piles of objects blocking the floor. They agreed that Yana would stay for three months to start with and they would both see how things progressed. Yana was to have a room rent-free in return for helping with decluttering, shopping, some cooking and housework and flute playing. Malory sat on her throne-like chair with Yana beside her holding a dozing Bertram, and they were soon talking about music and Malory's passion for Dusty Springfield. To her evident delight, Yana took out her flute and played *The Windmills of Your Mind.*

'She's a delightful lady. So elegant! Hopefully, you've made a good match here,' Cedric whispered to Swift.

'Fingers crossed. Worth a try and I thought it might be mutually beneficial. It gives Yana a chance to establish a life. And you get your sofa back.'

'Yes, and Oliver can visit again. He told me he would stay away while Yana was with me because, to quote, "He would feel he had to speak his mind." Astonishing, how narrow minded and self-righteous he can be.'

Cedric's uncertain tone chimed with Swift's immediate thought that Yana's move might prove a mixed blessing.

Malory was tapping her fingers on the chair arm, nodding to the music, her eyes lively. It was good to see her so animated. Yana had put on weight and was growing less timid as each day went by. She seemed to have grown taller, probably because she raised her head more frequently. Swift hoped that the arrangement would work out. If it succeeded, Yana might be able to enrol in college in the autumn and start to build a future.

He felt relieved but tired and was looking forward to his boat and the river. He was already imagining the sun and breeze and the flow of running water. His solitary heaven on earth. Time to unwind and clear his head of conflicts and betrayals, give his body something to think about other than scrapes and bruises.

His phone rang and he excused himself and went into the hall. He heard a voice he had only listened to once before, when there had been deep mutual enmity. It was frailer now, higher in pitch and the words came with huge effort.

'It's Emlyn here. Emlyn Williams. I thought I would want to know. Ruth's in labour, they have just taken her to hospital. The pains started about an hour ago. She is all right and as far as I know, the baby is too. Premature though, by a month.'

'I'm on my way. I'll text her.'

'Good, good. I'll stay at home, I won't go there. I'll wait here for news. I hope all will be well.'

Swift's mouth had gone dry. He returned to the living room.

'I have to go. My baby is on the way. Cedric, can I take the car?'

Cedric stood, swaying slightly. 'Of course, of course. But she's not due yet, surely?'

'No, it's too soon.'

'Off you go, quickly! I'll get a taxi home.'

'A father! You're going to be a father!' Malory said.

'I am, yes.'

He ran out and got into the car. He put his shaking hands on the wheel, steadying himself. He had no idea what it meant for a baby to be born at eight months. He felt ignorant, stupid and unprepared for what was to come. He texted Ruth: *On my way to the hospital now.*

He took a deep breath, turned the ignition and headed for Brighton.

THE END

Thank you for reading this book. If you enjoyed it please leave feedback on Amazon, and if there is anything we missed or you have a question about then please get in touch. The author and publishing team appreciate your feedback and time reading this book.

Our email is office@joffebooks.com

www.joffebooks.com

ALSO BY GRETTA MULROONEY

ARABY
MARBLE HEART
OUT OF THE BLUE
COMING OF AGE
LOST CHILD

TYRONE SWIFT BOOKS
THE LADY VANISHED
BLOOD SECRETS
TWO LOVERS, SIX DEATHS

Printed in Great Britain
by Amazon